7 BEST SHORT STORIES BY
LEO TOLSTOY

Tacet Books

7 BEST SHORT STORIES BY LEO TOLSTOY

Edited by
August Nemo

Editor August Nemo
Cover and Interior Design Mayra Falcini
Marketing Horacio Corral

Publisher's Cataloging-In-Publication Data (CIP)

Tolstoy, Leo
T654 7 best short stories by Leo Tolstoy / Leo Tolstoy – São Paulo, SP: Tacet Books, 2021.
171 p. : 14 x 21 cm

ISBN 978-65-991549-9-7

1. Russian literature.

CDD 891.7

Tacet Books
Made in silence
For noisy minds

www.tacetbooks.com
tacet.books@gmail.com

Contents

The Author

Lev Nikolaivich Tolstoi was born on September 9th, 1828, at his father's estate, Yasnaya Polyana, in the Government of Tula. His family is said to have been of German descent, originally bearing the somewhat plebeian name of Dick, which they changed for its Russian equivalent *Tolsty*, when they migrated to Muscovy at the beginning of the seventeenth century. The first eminent member of the stock was Peter Andrievich (1645–1727), one of Peter the Great's most famous "fledgelings," renowned for his energy, versatility, and diplomatic *finesse*, whom his master richly endowed and raised to countly rank. Yet Peter himself seems always to have stood on his guard against him. "Tolstoi," he is reported to have said, "is an able and intelligent man; but it is just as well, when you have anything to do with him, to have a good big stone handy, that you may be able to break his teeth in case it should suddenly occur to him to bite you." It was this sinister sleuth–hound who hunted down the unfortunate Tsarevich Alexis in his Neapolitan retreat, and thus drew down upon himself the well–merited hatred of the Russian people, who regarded the murdered Prince as a martyr for orthodoxy. Another ancestor, Peter Aleksandrevich (1769–1844), was a notable warrior, who, after fighting the Poles and Turks under Suvorov and Napoleon under Bennigsen, crushed the Polish revolt of 1831, and quitted the army with the rank of a Field–Marshal The Tolstois, though not belonging to the ancient Muscovite Boyar families themselves, have always held their heads high amomg the modern Russian aristocracy, and it used to be the boast of the family that not a single member of it had ever contracted a *misalliance,* Tolstoi's own mother was a Princess Volkhonskaya, his paternal grandmother was a Princess Gorchakova, his maternal grandmother was a Princess Trubetskoya, all three of them lineal descendants of Rurik, the antipatriarch of the Muscovite Tsars. Tolstoi himself had a strong outward resemblance to his grandfather, Prince Nicholas Volkhonsky (the prototype of Bolkonsby in "War and Peace"), though of a somewhat rougher build. Thus for two centuries the bluest of blood has coursed through the veins of the Tolstois, and though the present owner of Yasnaya Polyana has been in the habit of going about in peasant's garb, the portraits adorning the walls of the mansion represent, with scarcely an exception, counts, princes, and privy– counsellors, all bedizened with stars and ribbons.

Tolstoi's father, Count Nikolai Ilich, was described by those who knew him as a stately, fascinating personage. As Lieut– Colonel in the Pavlopadsky Regiment he had served with distinction throughout the epoch– making campaign of 1812– 1813. Nikolai Tolstoi inherited from his father an almost bankrupt estate, and as, after satisfying his father's creditors to the uttermost farthing, he found it impossible to subsist on his scanty pay, he resorted to the time– honored family practice of marrying a heiress, a lady of few personal charms but great wealth, considerably older than himself, Maria Ivanovna Volkhonskaya. Nevertheless this *mariage de convenance* proved an extremely happy though not a very lasting union, Tolstoi losing his mother when he was only three years of age (she died in 1831) and his father six years later. If, as is commonly supposed, Tolstoi's mother was the original of the Princess Maria in "War and Peace," she must, young as he was at the time of her death, have made a deep impression upon him. He describes her as of a tender, plaintive, mystical nature, of such finely woven texture as scarce to seem to belong to this world, one of those heroines of self– sacrifice who live not for themselves and "who do not so much, die as fly to Heaven." One precious gift she possessed, moreover, which her son certainly inherited from her, the gift of inventing tales and stories which held her hearers spellbound. It is said that when she was in a ballroom she quickly gathered round her a bevy of curious damsels who forgot their partners and everything else as they listened spellbound to the stories of the Princess Volkhonskaya.

Tolstoi's earliest reminiscences have thus been recorded by himself in a work published eight years ago. Perhaps no other great writer's memory has ever been able to travel so far back.

"These are my first recollections (which I cannot arrange in their proper sequence, not knowing which come first and which later, of some I cannot even say whether they were seen asleep or awake). Here, at any rate, they are: – I was tied up in a bundle, I wanted to stretch out my arms and I couldn't do it, and I cried and wept and my crying was disagreeable to myself, yet I couldn't leave off. Someone or other seemed to be bending over me. I don't remember who. And all this was happening in a semi– gloom. But I remember there were two persons present, and my crying had the same effect upon them; they were troubled by my crying, but they did not take me out of my bandages as I wanted them to do, and I cried all the louder. My being tied up seemed to them to be a necessary thing, whereas I knew that it was not necessary, and I wanted to prove it to them, and I spent myself in crying, and this crying was disagreeable to myself but unrestrainable, I felt the injustice and cruelty – not of people, for they had compassion on me, but of fate, and I felt pity for myself I know not and never could make out how exactly it was, that is to say, whether they had swathed me so when I was a suckling and I stretched out my arms, or whether they had swathed me when I was years older in order that I might not scratch myself. Whether, as is often the case in dreams, I concentrated many impressions in this one recollection I cannot say, but it is certain that this was my first and strongest impression of life. And what I remember about it most is not my crying, or my suffering, but the complicity, the contrariety of the impression. I wanted liberty, that liberty interfered with nobody, and I who wanted strength was weak while the others were strong.

"My second impression is a joyous one. I am sitting in a trough and surrounded by the novel and unpleasant odour of some substance or other with which my little body comes in contact. Possibly it was bran, and possibly this bran was in the water and the trough, but the novelty of the impression of the bran awoke my faculties, and for the first time I observed, and loved my little body with its ribs visible on its trunk, and the smooth dark trough and the bare arms of my nurse, and the warm, steamy, terrifying water and the sound of it, and, in particular, the sensation of the wetness of the smooth sides of the trough when I drew my tiny hands along it.

"It is strange and terrible to reflect that, from my birth to my third year, at the very time when I was being nourished at the breast, taken from the breast – at the very time when I was beginning to crawl, to walk, to speak – it is strange, I say, that, search my memory as I will, I can find therein no impressions whatever save these two.

"What was the beginning? When did I begin to live? . . . Did I not live indeed when I learnt to see, to hear, to speak, when I slept, sucked the breast and kissed the breast, and laughed and delighted my mother? I lived and lived gloriously! Did not I then acquire everything whereby I live now? – and did I not acquire so much so quickly, that in all the remainder of my life I have not acquired a hundredth part of what I acquired then? From a child of five to me, as I am now, is but a step. From a new– born child to a child of five the distance is terrific...

"The recollections which follow refer only to my fourth and fifth years, but even of these there are but few, and not one of them refers to life outside the walls of the house. Nature till my fifth year did not exist for me. All that I recollect occurs in my little bed and in my bedroom... People must have let me play with flowers, with leaves; they must needs have shielded me from the sun; but till my fifth or sixth year I have not a single recollection of what we call nature. Possibly one has to get away from her in order to see her, and I was nature.

"The next thing after my trough that I recollect is the recollection of Eremeevna. 'Eremeevna' was the word with which they used to frighten us children. No doubt they frightened us long before this, but my recollection of it is as follows: I am in my little bed, and very happy and comfortable, as I always was, and I should not have remembered anything about it, if the nurse or someone else who then made part of my life, had not said something or other in a voice new to me and went away, and at once a feeling of terror was added to the feeling of comfort. And I recollect that I was not alone, but someone else was there just like me. (This no doubt was my sister Mashenka, who was a year younger than myself, for our beds were in the same little room.) And I recollect there was a little curtain to my bed, and my sister and I were tremulously delighted at the extraordinary thing that was befalling us, and I kept on hiding my head in my pillow and glancing at the door from which I was expecting something novel and pleasant to emerge. And we laughed and hid our faces and waited. And behold! someone appeared in a gown and high cap such as I had never seen before, yet I recognised it to be the same person who was always with me (my nurse or my aunt, which I know not), and this someone spoke in a gruff voice, which I recognised, something terrible about naughty children and about Eremeevna. I trembled with fear and joy, I was terrified and yet delighted in my terror, and I wanted the someone who was frightening me not to know that I recognised her. We were silent, and after that we began to whisper together – our purpose was to conjure up Eremeevna again.

"I have another recollection similar to that of Eremeevna, and possibly later in time, because it is much clearer, although it has always remained unintelligible to me. In this recollection the principal part is played by a German called Theodor Ivanovich, our tutor, yet I know for certain that I was not under his control at the time, so this must have taken place before my fifth year. And this was my first impression of Theodor Ivanovich. And it was of so early occurrence that I still recollected nobody at that time, neither my brothers, nor my father. If I have any recollection at all of any particular person, it is only of my sister, and I only recollect her because she shared with me my terror of Eremeevna. Connected with this recollection is my first consciousness of the fact that our house had an upper storey. How I got up there, whether I went there myself, or whether someone carried me, I don't recollect at all. I only recollect that there were a good many of us there, and we were all dancing, holding each other's hands, and there were some strange women amongst us (I have a dim recollection that they were washerwomen), and we all began to leap and caper, and Theodor Ivanovich also leaped, lifting his feet too high and too noisily and boisterously, and the same instant I felt that this was not right but excessive, and I looked at him, and meseems I began to cry, and the whole thing came to an end.

"That is all I can recollect up to my fifth year. I remember nothing of my nurse, my aunts, my brothers, my sisters, my father, my rooms, and my games. My recollections grow more distinct from the time when they brought me downstairs to Theodor Ivanovich and to the older children.

"On being taken downstairs to Theodor Ivanovich and the children, I experienced for the first time, and consequently more strongly than at any subsequent period, the feeling which we call the sense of duty, the feeling of the cross which everyone is called upon to bear. It was painful to me to forsake what I had been accustomed to (accustomed to from eternity, as it then seemed to me); it was painful, poetically painful, to part not only from people, from my sister, my aunt, but also from my little bed with the curtains, from my little pillow, and frightful to me was the new life on which I was entering I tried to find pleasure in the new life which stood before me; I tried to believe in the endearing words with which Theodor Ivanovich enticed me to him; I tried not to perceive the contempt with which the other children received me, because I was smaller than they; I tried to think that it was a shame for a big boy to go on living with little girls, and there was no good at all in the life upstairs with my nurse; but at heart I was frightfully miserable, and I knew that I had lost beyond recall innocence and happiness, and only the feeling of my own dignity, the consciousness that I was doing my duty, sustained me.

"Many times, subsequently, in the course of my life it has been my lot to experience such moments at the turning–points of life as I turned into fresh paths. I have experienced a silent misery at irreparable losses. Whatever they may have said to me about going down to the other children, the chief thing I remember is the *khalat*[1] with the strap sewn on to the back, which they put on me so as to separate me for ever from the life upstairs, and then for the first time I observed not all those with whom I had lived upstairs hitherto, but the chief person with whom I lived and whom I did not remember before. This was my aunt, T. A. I remember her as a smallish, stout, dark– haired, kind, fresh, compassionate person. She dressed me in my *khalat,* fitted it round me, fastened my belt, and kissed me, and I saw that she felt the same thing as I did; she felt that it was sad, terribly sad, but necessary. I began to feel for the first time that life was not a game, but a serious affair . . ."[2]

Shortly before the death of Tolstoi's father, the whole family, consisting of four boys and one little girl, removed to Moscow in order that the eldest son, Nicholas, might prepare for the University, but the sudden death of Count Tolstoi, almost immediately afterwards, left the family in such straitened circumstances that they were obliged to return at once to Yasnaya Polyana, where the children were taught German by a German governess and Russian language and literature by a poor native seminarist. According to his Aunt Polina Yushkovaya, who was now responsible for his bringing up, little Lev had a petulant temper but an excellent heart, and was given to playing pranks of a somewhat disconcerting character. Between his seventh and eighth year he was possessed by the strange idea that he could fly if only he planted himself firmly on the soles of his feet, at the same time clasping his knees tightly enough, and he actually at-

1 A long jacket.

2 "Poslyednie Razskazui i Stat'i," Berlin, 1894.

tempted to carry his theory into practice by leaping in this peculiar posture from one of the top windows of the house, with the inevitable result of a broken leg. We also have a very full and interesting description of his later childhood in his first work, "Dyetsvo" ("Childhood"), published in a newspaper *Sovremennik,* in 1852, from which it is obvious that from a very early age he was an acute and impressionable observer. And here it may be remarked that nearly all Tolstoi's works are to a large extent autobiographical documents.

If Tolstois mother had some of the characteristics of a saint, as much cannot be said of his aunt and guardian, Polina Yushkovaya. She appears, from all accounts, to have been a good– natured, worldly minded woman, very proud of her great connexions, and considering wealth and position as the sole means to happiness. One of her favourite maxims was, nothing licks a young man into shape so much as a carefully contrived liaison with a woman *comme il* faut. *Nor were matters made much better when, in* the early forties, young Tolstoi went to Kazan to complete his education. It was usual in those days for the Russian youths to go direct to the University from their homes, where the teaching they got was, at best, very impecfect and perfunctory, instead of, as now, using the Gymnasium as a stepping– stone to the University. Moreover, the University curriculum of the period was not of a very superior character. Those were the iron days of Nicholas I., when an artfully organized system of repression dominated all things – education included. Every lecture and every examination– paper was carefully censured beforehand, and "even to Archbishops," as the Tsar himself expressed it, " the whole book could not possibly be given." Add to this that the University of Kazan itself was very much below the level of the Universities of St. Petersburg and Moscow. The life of the students at the old Volgan city is described by contemporaries as extremely stormy and scandalous. Princely students kept whole streets in a state of siege for weeks together by incessantly discharging air– guns from their garret– windows at all passers– by, and most of the aristocratic students formed exclusive little *coteries* among themselves which were so engrossed with really important matters like balls, picnics, dramatic entertainments, and very often less reputable forms of amusement; that they had very tittle time left for mere study. Moreover, this easy, pleasant state of existence came all the easier because Kazan, in those days, was the regular place of resort in the summer– time for the county families of the whole country side, who flocked thither to educate their sons and find husbands for their grown– up daughters. The higher classes, all mote or less closely connected, gloried in a large patriarchal hospitality, A young bachelor student of good family in those days need never keep his own table. Twenty or thirty houses were open to him daily without special invitation, he had only to pick and choose. A student, when once in the full swing of the thing, could rarely get to bed till five o'clock in the morning, and rarely rose till after twelve o'clock at noon. Tolstoi, in the character of "Nikolmka Irtenev" has given us a vivid piece of self– portraiture as he was at Kazan. A morbid sensitiveness, a pitiful lack of moral and mental equilibrium, a consuming pride; and a disgust at his own privileged position which points to a latent reserve of nobility, is legible in every line of this description, His plainness was evidently one of his sorest troubles. "I was bashful by nature," he tells us through the mouth of his hero; "but my bashfulness grew with the growing consciousness of my ugliness, . . . and like the fox who made believe that the grapes were sour, I affected to despise all the gratifications attainable by an agreeable exterior, and tried with all the strength of my mind and imagination to find delight in a haughty isolation." The unsatisfying futility of the butterfly– life he led filled him with a savage impatience. He could quite understand, be tells us, the commission of the greatest crimes, not from any desire to injure but from sheer curiosity to see what would happen, from the sheer necessity of doing something, "There are moments," he says, "when the future presents itself to our mind's eye in such dark colours that we fear to face it with the eye of reason, and try to persuade ourselves that there will be no Future and that there has been no Past. At such moments I can well understand a youth lighting a fire beneath the very house where his parents, his brothers and sisters, whom he tenderly loves, are sleeping; aye, and doing it without the least fear or hesitation and even with a smile upon his face" He was firmly convinced at this time that everyone, from his grandmother to his coachman, hated him and delighted in his sufferings and he took a melancholy pleasure in reflecting that this was to be his destined fate. Yet at this very time he was being petted and fêted by all his acquaintance, and allowed to have his own way in everything. The house of his Aunt Yushkovava was the most aristocratic in Kazan and young Tolstoi took case to frequent none but the best company, absolutely ignoring the existence of his poorer brethren in grey homespun. His habitual pose was truculent and defiant, his face contemptuous, and he made it a rule never to salute any of his fellow students who regarded him as a superior being simply because he wore a magnificent mantle trimmed with beaver and had a horse and a coachman at his disposal. Tolstoi himself divided the whole world into two classes: those who were *comme il faut* and those who were *comme il ne faut pas*. The characteristics of the *comme il faut* people were a correct pronunciation of French, well–kept nails, an aptitude for dancing and bowing elegantly, and above all an habitual expression of well– bred contemptuous *ennui*. The *comme il ne faut pas* people, who possessed none of these saving virtues, he heartily despised, while any person unfortunate enough to speak bad French instantly kindled within him a feeling of hatred. The moral tone of the distinguished circle in which he moved was low indeed. Looking back upon this melancholy period of his life at a later day he remarks (in his "Ispovyed" or Confession), that whenever he tried to be morally good he encountered contempt and laughter, but whenever he gave himself up to pleasant vices he was applauded and encouraged. His good aunt, whom he describes as "the purest of women," frequently told him that she desired nothing so much for him as a liaison with a married lady, and it was the dearest wish of her heart that he should become the Emperors adjutant, wed a rich girl, and have lots of slaves. Most of his brothers, according to Professor Zagoskin, showed no sign of moral restraint (especially Sergius, who subsequently ran away with a gipsy), with the exception of Demetrius, a mystical ascetic, who went to the opposite extreme, spent half his time on his knees, and could only be persuaded to go to a ball when the biblical example of King David, dancing before the Ark, was urged upon him. As for Lev Tolstoi himself, religion had so little weight with him at this time that when a casual companion lightly remarked that praying was both unnecessary and ridiculous, he cast aside the habit with as little concern as if he were simply "brushing a piece of fluff off his coat– sleeve." Under these circumstances it is scarcely surprising to learn that he learnt but little of value at Kazan. History he already despised as "a tissue of legends and trifles generally unnecessary and often immoral." The juridical Faculty he despised because all its professors were Germans. Finally, he attached himself to the Faculty of Oriental Tongues, one of the special features of the University of Kazan, but despite the extra aid of private instruction, was duly plucked at his examination. Finally, in 1847, he quitted Kazan and returned to the family estate at Yasnaya Polyana, where he resided for the next four years.

Even now young Tolstoi was painfully impressed by the wretched condition of the Russian muzhik, and anxious to ameliorate his lot. "Was it not my sacred and obvious duty," he cries[3]"to have a care for these 700 men, for whom I was responsible to God?" His earlier efforts in this direction, however, were defeated by the invincible laziness of the peasants and his own inexperience. It was about this time, moreover, that his humanitarian theories received a powerful impetus from a diligent study of Rousseau.

In 1851 Tolstoi received fresh impressions from a visit to the Caucasus with his brother Nicholas. After faffing down the Volga through the country of the Cabnucks, who then were still fire– worshippers, they settled down on the left bank of the Terek, not far from Kizylar, in the midst of a simple, unaffected people, spending most of their tune in shooting pheasants, hunting wild boars, and wandering through fen and forest The beauty and variety of the Caucasian scenery, where, in a few hours, one passes from the realm of eagles and mow– storms to emerald– green valleys where the dense oak forests are thick with azaleas and laurels, where myrtles and cypresses grow in the open air, and mountain ranges, dominated by the snowy caps of Elbrus and Kazbek, form an impressive background, powerfully affected

3 Speaking through the mouth of Prince Nekhlyudov, in "Utr Pomyeshchika," who is Tolstoi himself.

young Tolstoi. Nor was he without strange adventures and curious experiences. On one occasion he narrowly escaped capture at the hands of the savage mountaineers whilst on an excursion five miles from the nearest Russian outpost, and had to ride for his life. On another occasion he lost so heavily at cards that despairing of ever being able to pay his debts he resorted, in a sudden access of religious fervour, to the desperate expedient of prayer, and while still on his knees was interrupted by the arrival of an unexpected messenger from a friend with a gift of money. It is to this residence in the Caucasus that we owe one of the most brilliant and characteristic of Tolstoi's earlier works: "Kavkazsky Plyennik" ("The Captive in the Caucasus"), a later adaptation of which by Tolstoi himself forms No. 2 in the present collection.

At this period of his life Tolstoi was an enthusiastic hunter and full of martial fervour. He was easily persuaded to join the artillery, had several brushes with the enemy, and lived modestly on his pay of five roubles (ten shillings) a month, till he had paid off all his card debts. He passionately desired at this time to win the Cross of St George for valour (which is said to have been withheld from him, though well merited, by the enmity of his superior officer), and on the outbreak of the Crimean War was attached to the staff of the Commander– in– Chief, Count Gorchakov, determined at all hazards to win the laurels denied to him in the Caucasus. Throughout the war he distinguished himself, both as an officer and a soldier, by the most irreproachable valour, realising his own ideal[4] of true courage by doing his duty on every occasion without vain glory or desperation, and took an active part in the disastrous battle of the Black River. There can be lit-

4 As subsequently presented by Capt. Khlopov in "Nabyeg," and by Timokhin in "Voina i Mir."

tle doubt that the rude but salutary lessons of active warfare, teaching as it does to those who will learn the lesson, the urgent necessity of complete self– restraint and self– surrender, had a purifying, ennobling influence on Tolstoi's character. His comrades, in general, seem to have adored him. "Tolstoi," says one of them, "with his tales and couplets, enlivened us all. In the fullest sense of the word he was the soul of our party. When he was with us, time seemed to fly, and our merriment was endless; but when he was away all our noses hung down dismally enough." The couplets he composed on the occasion of the battle of August 4th were sung by the whole army; but his hopes of obtaining a field– adjutancy were dashed in consequence of some bitterly sarcastic verses on his official chiefs which he could not resist writing, and which when once written circulated in MS. from hand to hand. It was now, too, that he drafted the first sketch of his famous "Sevastopolskie Razskazui" ("Sebastopol Tales"), which, even in its rough form, drew tears from the Empress Alexandra, and induced Tsar Nicholas himself to remark that "the life of this young author must be looked after," and to order that he should be transferred to a less dangerous position.

At the end of 1855, on his return to St. Petersburg, the young and titled "hero of Sebastopol" found all the best houses open to him, while "The Sebastopol Tales" gave him the *entrée* to the leading literary circles. His earlier works, "Dyetsvo" ("Childhood"), first published in 1852 in the Sovremennik, where it was speedily followed by "Utro Pomyeshchika" and "Otrochestvo" ("Boyhood"), though highly spoken of by Nekrasov and other connoisseurs, do not seem to have attracted general attention. Now, however, he was regarded as one of the leading spirits of that new era of emancipation and enlightenment which coincided with the accession of the Tsar– Liberator, Alexander II. But Tolstoi was never able to thrive in literary circles. This was due not so much to his super– sensitiveness and natural reserve as to an intimate conviction, which he invariably expressed with the utmost frankness, that the cult of art and literature was mostly affectation and mere phrasing. He never would believe in the regenerating influence of mere culture. This was the secret of his quarrel with his great contemporary, Turgenev, whose cosmopolitanism, Anglomania, and "gentlemanly way of regarding literature and progress generally," absolutely revolted him. The Russian author, Fet', who met Tolstoi one evening at Nekrasov's, observed in him, at the very first instant, "an involuntary opposition to everything generally accepted in the department of criticism." In other words, young Tolstoi refused to believe in the dawn of a new era of progress in which poets and artists were to be the priests of culture, and show the people a new and better way. Such optimistic theories struck him as mere nostrums. But listen to his own account of the matter. "I began to doubt the truth of the theory because the priests of this new religion did not agree among themselves. I found that we had not made up our minds on the essential point, what is good and what is evil, so that we, the sole teachers of truth, attacked and contradicted one another like so many Bedlamites." For Tolstoi even now was against every sort of compromise. He aimed at nothing short of absolute perfection and at perfection alone. At the same time the desire to excel everyone in everything was strong within him Even physically it was his ambition to be stronger and more dexterous than his fellows, and he began a course of gymnastic exercises which even in his old age he was not altogether to abandon. We are told that on his return to Yasnaya

Polyana his steward coming to him in the morning for orders would frequently find his master hanging in flannels, head downwards, on a trapeze, in which position he would discuss the best modes of sowing and threshing, the steward accompanying his young master round and round the room as he turned somersaults without interrupting the conversation. Forty– five years later tihe habitual filling of a huge water– butt for domestic purposes was to be to him what the hewing down of trees used to be to Mr. Gladstone.

It was in 1856 that Tolstoi quitted the capital for the repose and seclusion of Yasnaya Polyana, dividing his time between agricultural pursuits (ploughing and sowing his own fields and labouring hard to better the condition of his serfs) and literature. To this period belong the novels and romances, – "Yunost" ("Youth"), "Vstryecha v Otryadye" (" The Encounter in the Battalion "), " Metel' " (" The Snowstorm "), No. 1 of the present collection, " Zapiski Markera " (" The Memories of a Marker "), and " Dva Husara" ("Two Hussars").

In 1857 Tolstoi went abroad for the first time, and was away for two years visiting Geranany, in which he was very much interested, and France. At Paris he again encountered Turgenev, but the meeting was anything but felicitous. Writing to a friend as to his experiences on this occasion, Turgenev remarks : " I cannot get on with Tolstoi anyhow, our views are so utterly different" Twelve months later Tolstoi went abroad again, but between his first and second foreign tour occurred what he always regarded as the tragedy of his life– the death of his elder brother Nicholas, to whom he was devotedly attached, and who is said to have been the one really intimate friend, except his wife, he ever possessed Turgenev describes the elder Tolstoi as u a talented talker and story–

teller, who always lived by himself either in the country or in quite impossible quarters at Moscow, sharing everything with the poor/' The effect of this bereavement upon Let was crushing. " Nothing in all my life," he tells us, " made such an impression upon me. Why worry and suffer any more, I thought to myself, when nought remains of such a one as Nikolai Nikolaevich? " From hence- forth the shadow of death falls across his finest pages, and he is possessed by a constantly deepening feeling of the futility of life and the emptiness of the best that it can offer. Even art lost its charm for him. " Art is a lie, and I cannot love a lie however beautiful, is his summing up of the whole matter. It was in this morbidly gloomy frame of mind that he wrote Lucerne " and " Albert," surely the most pessimistic productions of modern fiction.

Tolstoi's second Continental tour was a voyage of instruction. His alert, receptive, and thorough- going nature laid all branches of foreign learning under contributioa First he visited Berlin to attend the lectures of Droysen and Du Bois Raymond, and study the Prussian penal system, being a frequent visitor at the Moabit Prison, where the solitary confinement system chiefly occupied his attention. He also care- fully investigated the various trade unions founded by Schulze- Delitsch, and' made the acquaintance of the celebrated pedagogue Diesterweg, who struck him as somewhat " hard and dry." Thence he pro- ceeded to Dresden, where he diligently inspected all the principal schools, and paid a sudden and alarming visit on Auerbach, who happened at that time to be his favourite author. Tolstoi abruptly intro- duced himself as Eugen Bauman, one of Auerbach's characters ; but the author of the " Schwarzwalder Dorfgeschichten," was more frightened than flattered by the unlooked- for inroad of the grim, bizarre- looking young

Muscovite, and even Tolstoi's compliment, "Your books have made me think seriously of many things," did not immediately reassure him At first Auerbach seems to have taken him for a peasant from some remote village who had come either to abuse or to blackmail him for defamation of character. Passing from Dresden to Kissingen, Tolstoi made the acquaintance of Froebel, and then travelling slowly through Switzer– land, Italy, and France, proceeded via Brussels to London. It was during this period that he wrote " Tri Smerti " (" Three Deaths "), the last story in the present collection, " Semeinoe Schasti " (" Family Luck"), and " Polikushka."

Tolstoi returned from his second visit to the West full of educational ideas, which he instantly pro– ceeded to put into practice. He began to publish a pedagogic journal, entitled Yasnaya Polyana, from the name of his estate, and started a school for the children of his peasantry – the first free school that ever existed in Russia, which was absolutely unique of its kind. Tolstoi adopted the two– fold principle that " all constraint is dangerous and argues want of proper method," and that " teachers ought to consult not their own convenience but the convenience of their pupils." Accordingly his pupils were allowed practically to do as they liked They could come and go at will, might sit on chairs huddle into corners, or stand at the window with their backs to their teachers as the mood took them, and no discipline of any sort was countenanced. To interest the pupils while they taught them was to be the sole aim of their schoolmasters. This school created some little sensation in its day. French savants and experts raised their hands to Heaven in amazement, and professed they could not understand how order could be evolved from the midst of anarchy; and when the school payed their superior insight the bad compliment of actually succeeding, they could only explain the marvel by emphasizing the difference of temperament between lively French children and the more phlegmatic Slavs. In Russia itself some of the higher officials were uncomfortably agitated by Tolstoi's revolutionary pedagogic methods. The Minister of the Interior, an inveterate adherent of the old non– progressive school, complained to his colleague, the Minister of Education (October 14th, 1862), that, in his opinion, the school of Yasnaya Polyana, and the journal of the same name, threatened to undermine the very foundations of religion and morality, especially as the director and editor was "endowed with a remarkable, I may even say, attractive literary style." Moreover, laments the much perturbed official, Count Tolstoi's convictions are so evidently sincere as to place his motives above suspicion, so that there is absolutely no getting at him And yet opinions so eccentric were bound to mislead the unwary. What then was to be done? Fortunately, the Minister of Education, an enlightened liberal, could assure his colleague that he had carefully examined Count Tolstoi's m e t h ods, and convinced himself that they were worthy rather of praise than of censure, and although be, the Minister, could not say that he agreed with all the Count's views, he felt bound to thank and was determined to support him. Nevertheless the school soon died a natural death. Pupils were at first attracted by its novelty, but decamped the moment they felt they had learnt enough, and the attempt to found fourteen establishments of the same sort in other jdaces foiled for want of public support, where– upon Tolstoi abandoned the scheme altogether, and buried himself in the steppes inhabited by die nomadic Bashkirs, in order to "breathe fresh air, drink kumiss, and five the healthy, natural life of the brute beast" To this residence among the Bashkirs we are indebted for that piercingly vivid story; "How much land does a man want?" which win be found in toy former volume of selections entitled "Tales from Tolstoi"

Tolstoi presently exchanged the rough hospitality of the nomadic Bashkirs for the comfort of a home of his own. On September 23rd, 1862, he married Sophia Behr, the second daughter of a Moscow physician. The bride was eighteen, the groom four– afld– tfatrty, and at first the lady was not only indifferent to her wooer, but took no pains to conceal the fact It seems to have been a point of honour with the Behr family that the three daughters should be married in order of seniority, and they took it quite amiss when Tolstoi, passing over the eldest daughter, set his heart upon the second. The gentleman's final declaration, which was ultimately successful, is minutely described in "Anna Karenina," where Kitty Shcherbatskaya is Miss Behr, while Tolstoi has described himself to the life in the character of Levin. This union proved to be of the happiest, and was blessed with nine children, five boys and four girls, the youngest of whom was born in 1891. With his marriage the most joyous period of Tolstoi's life begins. Writing to a friend on October 9th, 1862, he says: " I have been married a fortnight, and I am a happy, a new, an altogether new man. My wife regularly looks after the cash and the acounts, and I have the bees, the sheep, a new garden, and the vines on my hands. Everything goes on pretty well, though of course it is not ideally perfect My wife is no doll She is of real help to me." His happiness is so great that it strikes him as being unnatural, but he consoles him– self with the reflection that love becomes purer and stronger beneath the threats of despair! On another occasion, however, he admits, without reserve, that he is perfectly happy in his married life. He has dis– covered that Fanny is not only a loving wife but an excellent mother; and a helper even in his literary work. The advent of children of his own gave him an opportunity of thoroughly applying his pedagogic theories to the great problem of their education.

Playthings were banished from the nursery, but the children were allowed the utmost liberty, being never chastised corporally, and brought up as closely as possible beneath the eyes of their parents. Assum– ing that nowhere was the independence of children so liberally provided for as in England, Tolstoi committed his own children, between the age of three and nine, to the care of an English governess. The young people were strictly forbidden «ver to com– mand the servants, but to say "if you please" for everything they wanted, their parents setting them the example in this respect The first symptom of lying was severely repressed by confining the offender to his room or putting him into Coventry, but the slightest sign of penitence was requited by instant forgiveness. The children were always with their parents except at meal times, or when they retired to rest, and the servants to whose charge they were then entrusted, were strictly cautioned to respect their innocence both by word and deed. We have it on the authority of one of Tolstoi's housekeepers that he was a first– rate manager. He saw to everything personally, negligence and slovenliness were im– possible under such a master. The smallest detail was not beneath his notice. His pig– stys, his cowsheds, andjstable were models of cleanliness. In his pigs he took particular pride. There were three hundred of them in all, and they lived in couples in separate stys. As for the dwelling– house, not a speck of dirt was allowed to settle there, the walls and floors had to be washed down every day. He would storm and rage if the least thing were neglected, and when his doctor remonstrated with him on the violence of his temper as likely to prove injurious to his health, Tolstoi, like Peter the Great before him, would declare that it was his nature. "I want to control myself but cannot," he would always say. His industry and economy were promptly rewarded by prosperity. Count Tolstoi's estate was one of the comparatively few in Russia of the same size which more than paid its expenses. Yasnaya Polyana was especially famous for its excellent cream, which sold in the Moscow market at 60 kopecks (is. 2#d) per pound. No description, we are told, can give any idea of the cheerful and attractive life at Yasnaya Polyana during the first sixteen years of Tolstoi's happy married life (1 862– 1 878). There was no subject, from cricket and football to the most abstruse branches of philosophy, in which Tolstoi did not take a lively interest, and though his acquaintances were few, they numbered among them some of the most enlightened and inter– esting men in Russia, including N. N. Strakhov, Prince Urusov, and the mathematician, A. Fet. As his sons grew up they became his closest companions. At his call they would joyfully come running out to join him in his long rambles (he rarely went a shorter distance than twelve miles at a stretch), or in a course of Swedish gymnastics, or compete with him at hurdle racing, or go a– hunting or shooting. In the winter the father and sons would be skating or sledging together, or bombarding snow fortifications of their own construction. Indeed Tolstoi asked for nothing better than to pass his days in the bosom of his family. He hated to be away from his wife and children even for a single day, and hastened back to them with rapture when the detaining business had been happily transacted. It was at this time of his life that an acquaintance said of him that he was laughing all day long.

But Tolstoi had other and more serious work during the long winter evenings. It was in the midst of this period of supreme domestic felicity that his two immortal masterpieces, " War and Peace " and " Anna Karenina," were composed

"Voina i Mir" ("War and Peace ") was begun immediately after his marriage, under the happiest auspices, and was completed in five years. That such a stupendous work, a whole library in itself, should have been composed within such a compara– tively short time is sufficiently surprising, but our surprise becomes amazement when we learn that the author actually transcribed its thousands of pages with his own hand seven times before he was satisfied with it With the possible exception of Turgenev's " Otsui i Dyeti" ("Fathers and Sons") five j'ears earlier no other Russian book ever created such a sensation. Despite its obvious defects (defects far less discer– nible, however, in the original than the translations be they never so good), prolixity, an almost total absence of humour and a disposition to philosophize a la Schopenhauer, under whose fascination Tolstoi lay at that particular time[5] "Voina i Mir" must ever rank amongst the few supremely great masterpieces of the world's literature. It i9 a prose epic of vast dimensions, the history of the life and death struggle of the whole Russian nation with its most terrible adversary the first Napoleon, for the Russian nation is the real hero of the romance, even the leading characters, Kutuzov and Platon Karataev, being mere idealised exponents or representatives of the

5 On August 30th, 1869, Tolstoi wrote to a friend: "I have an indescribable enthusiasm for Schopenhauer, who has given me a succession of intellectual delights, the like of which I have never experienced before. I know not, of course, whether my opinions may not change, but I am confident at present that Schopenhauer is the greatest of geniuses . . . and I can only attribute his being so little known to the fact that the world at large is made up of mere idiots."

nation at large. Yet when Tolstoi forgets the philosopher in the artist, and condescends to probe the personal characters of the protagonists in the terrible struggle, he convinces as no other great writer has ever suc– ceeded in convincing. The character of Napoleon is of itself a revelation. A great critic has well said that after reading the description of Alexander's interview with Bonaparte at Tilsit, one cannot rid oneself of the conviction that Tolstoi must have been concealed somewhere in the same room, for nowhere else do we seem to see " the little corporal " so vividly in the flesh as in the pages of " Voina i Mir." The philosophy of the book, as already hinted, i9 not without a tinge of Schopenhauerisia Thus, man's reason, coupled with his exacting egoism^ is held to be the source of all human suffering. The main duty of man is self– renunciation and absolute sub– jection to the will of the mass of humanity which makes up the nation. Kutuzov was a great man simply because he understood this, and had no independent will of his own. Such a system neces– sarily postulates the non– existence of separate human individuality, and, logically pursued, would make un– conscious instinct the best, because the strongest force in nature. Even religion is discarded, because, as Tolstoi plainly perceived, religion strengthens the sense of individuality by making man self– conscious. This after all is " Die Welt in Wille und Vorstellung " in a nutshell. No wonder, then, if Tolstoi's great con– temporary, Dostoevsky, after reading " Voina i Mir," put the book down with the simple remark : " The fool hath said in his heart there is no God." Yet Tolstoi himself at a later day was to reject Schopenhauer's philosophy as inadequate.

Tolstoi himself, at least while actually engaged upon the work,. was not a little proud of "Voina i Mir." " I regard all that I have printed hitherto," he wrote to a friend, " as mere trial– work for my pen." The first volume appeared in 1867, tihe last in 1869. The work of preparatory research tried Tolstoi severely. " You have no idea," he wrote to Fet in Noveniber, '69, " how difficult the initial labour of deep ploughing in the field where I am obliged to sow has been to me . . . ' Ars longa, vita brevis/ I think to myself every day."

After completing " Voina i Mir," Tolstoi set about writing a romance of the age of Peter the Great, and began collecting and arranging his materials with his usual energy and conscientiousness. " Dear little Le fr," wrote his wife on this occasion, " is surrounded by piles of book, portraits, and pictures, and sits reading and writing and re– writing with puckered brows. In the evening when the children have gone to bed he tells me of his plans."[6] But after five years of labour Tolstoi abandoned the idea altogether, because he had arrived at an estimate of Peter's character diametrically opposite to that which generally obtains, and discovered that he had no sympathy whatever with the Petrine period itself. " Not only do I find nothing great in the personality and the acts of Peter I., but I find that everything on the contrary was very bad," writes Tolstoi. " In all his so– called reforms he only looked after his own personal profit and not after the " interests of the State. In consequence of his disagree– ment with the Boyars as to his reforms, he founded St. Petersburg simply in order to be further away from them and to live his immoral life more freely? The sentence I have under– lined is a characteristic specimen of Tolstoi's unconscious one– sidedness, and of his inability to do justice to systems antagonistic to his own. Peter the Great undoubtedly transferred his capital to St. Petersburg in order to be further

6 While in the throes of composition Tolstoi demanded absolute quiet, not even his wife being allowed to interrupt him.

away from his Boyars. But why? Because he rightly perceived that reactionary Moscow would inevitably throw obstacles in the way of the reforms he judged to be indispensable to the civilising of ignorant and superstitious Russia, whereas St Petersburg, with the command of the sea, was a window thrown open to the humanizing influences of the West The prospect of greater license on the Neva than on the Moskva never entered into Peter's thoughts. Peter was always and everywhere frankly sensual; his strong sexual instincts had no rfespect whatever for either persons or places.

I suspect myself that Tolstoi's real quarrel with Peter was due to the fact that the great Tsar was an unanswerable confutation of the novelist's pet theory of the uselessness of independent individuality, for if ever a man was superior to his age and his environment, and moulded them both to his will, it was Peter the Great And yet there is a moral grandeur in Tolstoi's refusal to admire the exploits of the great national regenerator who owed so much of his success to the unflinching application of mere brute force. Mere achievement, however impressive, could never blind Tolstoi to the absence of moral greatness. We cannot, for instance, imagine him making a hero of a successful political freebooter like Frederick II. of Prussia.

" Anna Karenina," Tolstoi's second great work (his greatest in the opinion of many), was written between 1873 and 1876. The first seven parts appeared originally in the leading Moscow magazine, Russky Vyestnik, which, under the editorship of the eminent publicist, Michael Katkov, was a power in Russia. When, however, Katkov objected to certain portions of the eighth part of " Anna Karenina," which was diametrically opposed to his reactionary views, Tolstoi was greatly incensed, and cancelled his engagement with Katkov. " How dare a mere journalist alter a single line of my work?" he cried Tolstoi indeed never had any great love for newspapers or gazettes. "I never read anything but classics/' he once replied to a person who inquired what he usually read Yet very few classics really satisfied him. It was only after considerable hesitation that he allowed that that incomparable master of style, Pushkin, for instance, deserved the name of a classic at all, and even then Tolstoi was never tired of accusing the author of "Eugene Onyegin" of an excessive lightness of touch and a tendency to sacrifice truth and even intelligibility to brilliant and dramatic effects. Goethe, too, was never one of his favourites. " Righteous God ! " he cried, with an emphasis that was anything but profane, " Goethe always forgets morality in his pursuit of beauty, and without the former the latter is "worth nothing." In 1870 he "Began to study Greek and would read nothing else. Xenophon greatly pleased him, but he was still more delighted with Homer. " How glad I am that God has given me the humour for it," he writes to a friend ; "I am convinced that of all the truly beautiful, the simply beautiful which the human mind has pro– duced, I hitherto knew nothing." Of his own literary work he was still very proud, and yet his complacency was not without a tinge of self– contempt In 1876 he wrote to a friend, " I continue under the delusion that what I am writing is very important, although I know that within a month the remembrance of it will be on my conscience. Sometimes I feel myself to be as a God from whom nothing is concealed, and at other times I am as stupid as a brute beast." It pleased him to reflect that he was already numbered amongst the greatest of Russian writers, and it is certain that from 1880 onwards he was without a rival in the national literature. In the fifties Turgenev had been in the ascendant; in the sixties he had been obliged to share that distinction with Ostrovsky and Pisemsky; in the seventies the satirist, Saltuikov, and the most Russian of all the Russian novelists, Dostoevsky, held the public ; but five years after the publication of "Anna Karenina," Tolstoi had dis– tanced every competitor, and was undeniably supreme. And, characteristically enough, just as he had reached the height of his glory, doubts began to arise in his mind whether, to use a common phrase, the game was really worth the candle. Except for a very brief period in his youth Tolstoi had always despised mere style and had resolutely refused to cultivate the mere prettinesses of literature ; but now he began to doubt whether literature itself, like art, as to which he had already made up his mind, was not a vain, worthless, and even pernicious pursuit. " On reflecting upon the fame I should gain from my writings," he tells us, " I said to myself : Good ! supposing you become more famous even than Gogol, than Pushkin, than Shakes– peare, than Molifere, than all the great writers of the world, what then? And I could find' nothing to say, absolutely nothing. . . . Some indefinable power drove me towards the idea of ridding myself of life somehow or other. Indeed, the thought of suicide became so attractive that I had to use artifice against it so as not immediately to put it into execution. And this happened to me when I was completely happy, In his youth Tolstoi took some pains to cultivate an elegant and beautiful style, which is seen at its best in " Kazaki " (" The Cossacks "), published in 1 86 1. Yet there can be little doubt that his later style, so noble, simple, clear, poignant, and precise, with a constantly underlying suggestion of vast elemental power, is far more impressive. when I had absolutely everything I wanted!: a handsome family, ample means, fame constantly increasing, the respect of my neighbours, health, strength of mind and body, apparently everything. So long as I fancied life had some meaning in it, although I knew not how to express it, the reflection of life in art gave me pleasure, and it was pleasant to me to look upon life in this mirror called art But when I tried to discover the meaning of it all, the mirror struck me as tantalizing, or as simply nothing at all." This was in 1 88 1. Evidently a mental and moral crisis was approaching. Twenty years previously he had been t^mented by similar doubts, and, after much torturing self– analysis, had come to the conclusion that his writings were of no use to the people at large (in his mind the sole true test of their utility), and simply the product of egoism and self– glorification. " It is plain to me," he wrote in 1861, " that the compiling of magazines and books, the immense and ceaseless process of printing and publishing may be profitable enough for authors, printers, and publishers, but bring no benefit to the people, and therefore stands self– condemned." But then he had married. The happiness of a well– assorted match and a tranquil family life drew him quite away from all seeking after a general theory of life, and, as Tolstoi himself characteristically puts it, " although I considered all writing to be rubbish, I went on writing, nevertheless, for I had tasted of the seduction of writing, the seduction of the enormous literary renown of work which was really worthless."

But now, after an interval of twenty years, all the old doubts and misgivings had returned with tenfold force, and Tolstoi was powerless to resist them. Utterly dissatisfied with the life he was living, convinced that it was both " senseless and terrible," he looked about him for something which would better satisfy his heart and conscience. First he turned to Science, only to receive an interminable quantity of dark answers to questions he had never asked, but as to the meaning of life he did not receive, and of course could not receive any answer, for Science does not and cannot occupy herself with such a question. Next he applied to Philosophy, but Philosophy could but tell him that the only way out of life was through death. Finally, he arrived at the conclusion that Faith was the one mainstay of life – but where was Faith to be found? To acquire knowledge is easy, but to acquire faith when you have none within you seemed well– nigh impossible. In this dilemma Tolstoi began by consorting with monks and pilgrims, by frequenting the Optinsky monastery, by shutting him– self in his own room for private prayer, studying the Scriptures, and consulting Catholics, Protestants, and Raskolniks indiscriminately. He even took lessons in Hebrew from the Chief Rabbi of Moscow – and all without being able to arrive at any conclusion. " I had lived in the world five– and– fifty years, ,, he pathetically confesses, "and during all that time, excluding fourteen or fifteen childish years, I had lived as a Nihilist in the completest sense of the word, that is to say, not as a socialist or a revolutionist, as the word is commonly understood, but as one who had no faith, who had nothing. Science and Philosophy tell us that we must go on living as we are, in the firm belief that, according to the law of historical progress, after living for a long time badly, our life will right itself and suddenly become good of its own accord." We all know how the crisis ended We all know hov? Tolstoi found peace at last by resolutely devoting his whole life to labouring for the people in the spirit of the Sermon on the Mount. " Live according to faith, and faith will come to you," was his eureka. His eccentric, arbitrary, and – there is really no other word for it – his absurd mutilation of Scripture, which he was forced to recast in order to make it fit in with his own very peculiar version of the Gospels (as to which by the way he dog– matizes every whit as magisterially as the church which he so hastily disparaged and which was finally driven to condemn him), are too well known to be alluded to here. But however we may deplore Tolstoi's provocative method of biblical interpretation, we cannot but reverence the sublime unselfishness of the life he has led ever since what we may perhaps call his conversion. From 1 88 1 to the present time, he has literally devoted himself, body and soul, to the service of his poorer brethren, the Russian muzhiks, for whom he has always had an intense sympathy and admiration. He has done this in two ways, by working among them and by writing for them. He had always been of the opinion that " the only really honest labour worthy of a man was manual labour," and from henceforth he adopted the life of a common peasant, and worked vigorously alongside his labourers in his own fields.

"It is better," he observes, with equal wisdom and humanity, u it is better to help the poor by actually working at their own handicraft with them, than doing higher and perhaps more lucrative work, and giving them the profits thereof, inasmuch as by working with them you teach them to respect their own particular work by showing them that you yourself do not despise it, whereas any money you might give them would be apt to make them indolent and lazy." So he set about tilling his own fields, thatching his own cottage roofs and teaching his peasantry thrift smd economy by his own personal exampte. Nor was this all During the terrible winter of 1891– 92, when whole provinces of the Russian Empire presented the terrible and pathetic spectacle of an entire agricul– tural population, overwhelmed by snow, dying in thousands, without a word of complaint, though absolutely deprived of food, clothes, or firewood, Tolstoi hastened to the afflicted districts, and fed thousands daily at his own expense at improvised ordinaries, never quitting his post for a single instant till all danger was at an end Indeed, but for his indefatigable efforts, whole parishes would have been depopulated. Nor was this the first time that Tolstoi had shown himself the benefactor of the people. Some ten years before, when a terrible famine was raging in the Province of Samara, which calamity, apparently for economical reasons, was not " officially recognised," Tolstoi collected subscriptions for the relief of the dying peasantry, and, energetically aided by Katkov and the Moscow Gazette, never ceased calling attention to the catastrophe till he actually compelled the reluctant Government tardily to do its duty and mitigate a disaster it could no longer deny.

But perhaps Tolstoi has done even greater service to his beloved muzhiks with his pen than with his purse. Between 1880 and 1896 he composed for their benefit that series of simple, touching stories, so truly humane, so deeply Christian, and also, despite his own intentions, such exquisite masterpieces of realistic art in the truest sense of the word, some of the best of which were selected to form my former volume: "Tales from Tolstoi." We learn from his letter to Dembinsky in 1886, what moved Tolstoi thus to cater for the humblest of his readers : " These millions of poor Russians who just know their letters stand before us like so many hungry little daws with wide– open mouths crying to us : Gospoda native writers ! throw into these mouths of ours spiritual food worthy of you and us, nourish us hungry ones with the living literary word!' – And the simple and honest Russian people deserves that we should respond to its call."

During the years immediately preceding the publication of these further translations Tolstoi lived for the most part at Yasnaya Polyana, in the bosom of his family, working with and for his tenants continually, and yet finding time to answer daily the thousands of letters which reached him from all parts of the world, asking for his counsel and assistance m every imaginable sort of difficulty. He has been, with perhaps the single exception of Fr. John of Cronstadt, indisputably the most popular personage in the Empire of the Tsar. In the winter he generally resides at Moscow, frequenting, by preference, chari– table institutions and working men's concerts, despite his advanced age taking the liveliest interest in every question of the day, especially those relating to religion and morality, and delighting everyone by the alertness of his intelligence and the generous breadth of his sympathy. In 1899 the veteran astonished and delighted the world of literature with his " Voskresenie " (" Resurrection "), a noble work (despite its occasional extravagances) from every point of view, worthy of his best days, demonstrating that the hand of the master had lost none of its cunning, and piercing with the divination of genius to the deepest depths of human impulse and motive.

R. Nisbet Bain.[7]

7 Robert Nisbet Bain (1854-1909) was a British historian and linguist who worked for the British Museum.

God Sees the Truth, But Waits

In the town of Vladimir lived a young merchant named Ivan Dmitrich Aksionov. He had two shops and a house of his own.

Aksionov was a handsome, fair– haired, curly– headed fellow, full of fun, and very fond of singing. When quite a young man he had been given to drink, and was riotous when he had had too much; but after he married he gave up drinking, except now and then.

One summer Aksionov was going to the Nizhny Fair, and as he bade good– bye to his family, his wife said to him, "Ivan Dmitrich, do not start to– day; I have had a bad dream about you."

Aksionov laughed, and said, "You are afraid that when I get to the fair I shall go on a spree."

His wife replieWd: "I do not know what I am afraid of; all I know is that I had a bad dream. I dreamt you returned from the town, and when you took off your cap I saw that your hair was quite grey."

Aksionov laughed. "That's a lucky sign," said he. "See if I don't sell out all my goods, and bring you some presents from the fair."

So he said good– bye to his family, and drove away.

When he had travelled half– way, he met a merchant whom he knew, and they put up at the same inn for the night. They had some tea together, and then went to bed in adjoining rooms.

It was not Aksionov's habit to sleep late, and, wishing to travel while it was still cool, he aroused his driver before dawn, and told him to put in the horses.

Then he made his way across to the landlord of the inn (who lived in a cottage at the back), paid his bill, and continued his journey.

When he had gone about twenty– five miles, he stopped for the horses to be fed. Aksionov rested awhile in the passage of the inn, then he stepped out into the porch, and, ordering a samovar to be heated, got out his guitar and began to play.

Suddenly a troika drove up with tinkling bells and an official alighted, followed by two soldiers. He came to Aksionov and began to question him, asking him who he was and whence he came. Aksionov answered him fully, and said, "Won't you have some tea with me?" But the official went on cross– questioning him and asking him. "Where did you spend last night? Were you alone, or with a fellow– merchant? Did you see the other merchant this morning? Why did you leave the inn before dawn?"

Aksionov wondered why he was asked all these questions, but he described all that had happened, and then added, "Why do you cross– question me as if I were a thief or a robber? I am travelling on business of my own, and there is no need to question me."

Then the official, calling the soldiers, said, "I am the police– officer of this district, and I question you because the merchant with whom you spent last night has been found with his throat cut. We must search your things."

They entered the house. The soldiers and the police– officer unstrapped Aksionov's luggage and searched it. Suddenly the officer drew a knife out of a bag, crying, "Whose knife is this?"

Aksionov looked, and seeing a blood– stained knife taken from his bag, he was frightened.

"How is it there is blood on this knife?"

Aksionov tried to answer, but could hardly utter a word, and only stammered: "I– don't know– not mine." Then the police– officer said: "This morning the merchant was found in bed with his throat cut. You are the only person who could have done it. The house was locked from inside, and no one else was there. Here is this blood– stained knife in your bag and your face and manner betray you! Tell me how you killed him, and how much money you stole?"

Aksionov swore he had not done it; that he had not seen the merchant after they had had tea together; that he had no money except eight thousand rubles of his own, and that the knife was not his. But his voice was broken, his face pale, and he trembled with fear as though he went guilty.

The police– officer ordered the soldiers to bind Aksionov and to put him in the cart. As they tied his feet together and flung him into the cart, Aksionov crossed himself and wept. His money and goods were taken from him, and he was sent to the nearest town and imprisoned there. Enquiries as to his character were made in Vladimir. The merchants and other inhabitants of that town said that in former days he used to drink and waste his time, but that he was a good man. Then the trial came on: he was charged with murdering a merchant from Ryazan, and robbing him of twenty thousand rubles.

His wife was in despair, and did not know what to believe. Her children were all quite small; one was a baby at her breast. Taking them all with her, she went to the town where her husband was in jail. At first she was not allowed to see him; but after much begging, she obtained permission from the officials, and was taken to him. When she saw her husband in prison– dress and in chains, shut up with thieves and criminals, she fell down, and did not come to her senses for a long time. Then she drew her children to her, and sat down near him. She told him of things at home, and asked about what had happened to him. He told her all, and she asked, "What can we do now?"

"We must petition the Czar not to let an innocent man perish."

His wife told him that she had sent a petition to the Czar, but it had not been accepted.

Aksionov did not reply, but only looked downcast.

Then his wife said, "It was not for nothing I dreamt your hair had turned grey. You remember? You should not have started that day." And passing her fingers through his hair, she said: "Vanya dearest, tell your wife the truth; was it not you who did it?"

"So you, too, suspect me!" said Aksionov, and, hiding his face in his hands, he began to weep. Then a soldier came to say that the wife and children must go away; and Aksionov said good– bye to his family for the last time.

When they were gone, Aksionov recalled what had been said, and when he remembered that his wife also had suspected him, he said to himself, "It seems that only God can know the truth; it is to Him alone we must appeal, and from Him alone expect mercy."

And Aksionov wrote no more petitions; gave up all hope, and only prayed to God.

Aksionov was condemned to be flogged and sent to the mines. So he was flogged with a knot, and when the wounds made by the knot were healed, he was driven to Siberia with other convicts.

For twenty– six years Aksionov lived as a convict in Siberia. His hair turned white as snow, and his beard grew long, thin, and grey. All his mirth went; he stooped; he walked slowly, spoke little, and never laughed, but he often prayed.

In prison Aksionov learnt to make boots, and earned a little money, with which he bought The Lives of the Saints.

He read this book when there was light enough in the prison; and on Sundays in the prison– church he read the lessons and sang in the choir; for his voice was still good.

The prison authorities liked Aksionov for his meekness, and his fellow– prisoners respected him: they called him "Grandfather," and "The Saint." When they wanted to petition the prison authorities about anything, they always made Aksionov their spokesman, and when there were quarrels among the prisoners they came to him to put things right, and to judge the matter.

No news reached Aksionov from his home, and he did not even know if his wife and children were still alive.

One day a fresh gang of convicts came to the prison. In the evening the old prisoners collected round the new ones and asked them what towns or villages they came from, and what they were sentenced for. Among the rest Aksionov sat down near the newcomers, and listened with downcast air to what was said.

One of the new convicts, a tall, strong man of sixty, with a closely– cropped grey beard, was telling the others what be had been arrested for.

"Well, friends," he said, "I only took a horse that was tied to a sledge, and I was arrested and accused of stealing. I said I had only taken it to get home quicker, and had then let it go; besides, the driver was a personal friend of mine. So I said, 'It's all right.' 'No,' said they, 'you stole it.' But how or where I stole it they could not say. I once really did something wrong, and ought by rights to have come here long ago, but that time I was not found out. Now I have been sent here for nothing at all... Eh, but it's lies I'm telling you; I've been to Siberia before, but I did not stay long."

"Where are you from?" asked some one.

"From Vladimir. My family are of that town. My name

is Makar, and they also call me Semyonich."

Aksionov raised his head and said: "Tell me, Semyonich, do you know anything of the merchants Aksionov of Vladimir? Are they still alive?"

"Know them? Of course I do. The Aksionovs are rich, though their father is in Siberia: a sinner like ourselves, it seems! As for you, Gran'dad, how did you come here?"

Aksionov did not like to speak of his misfortune. He only sighed, and said, "For my sins I have been in prison these twenty– six years."

"What sins?" asked Makar Semyonich.

But Aksionov only said, "Well, well– I must have deserved it!" He would have said no more, but his companions told the newcomers how Aksionov came to be in Siberia; how some one had killed a merchant, and had put the knife among Aksionov's things, and Aksionov had been unjustly condemned.

When Makar Semyonich heard this, he looked at Aksionov, slapped his own knee, and exclaimed, "Well, this is wonderful! Really wonderful! But how old you've grown, Gran'dad!"

The others asked him why he was so surprised, and where he had seen Aksionov before; but Makar Semyonich did not reply. He only said: "It's wonderful that we should meet here, lads!"

These words made Aksionov wonder whether this man knew who had killed the merchant; so he said, "Perhaps, Semyonich, you have heard of that affair, or maybe you've seen me before?"

"How could I help hearing? The world's full of rumours. But it's a long time ago, and I've forgotten what I heard."

"Perhaps you heard who killed the merchant?" asked Aksionov.

Makar Semyonich laughed, and replied: "It must have

been him in whose bag the knife was found! If some one else hid the knife there, 'He's not a thief till he's caught,' as the saying is. How could any one put a knife into your bag while it was under your head? It would surely have woke you up."

When Aksionov heard these words, he felt sure this was the man who had killed the merchant. He rose and went away. All that night Aksionov lay awake. He felt terribly unhappy, and all sorts of images rose in his mind. There was the image of his wife as she was when he parted from her to go to the fair. He saw her as if she were present; her face and her eyes rose before him; he heard her speak and laugh. Then he saw his children, quite little, as they: were at that time: one with a little cloak on, another at his mother's breast. And then he remembered himself as he used to be– young and merry. He remembered how he sat playing the guitar in the porch of the inn where he was arrested, and how free from care he had been. He saw, in his mind, the place where he was flogged, the executioner, and the people standing around; the chains, the convicts, all the twenty– six years of his prison life, and his premature old age. The thought of it all made him so wretched that he was ready to kill himself.

"And it's all that villain's doing!" thought Aksionov. And his anger was so great against Makar Semyonich that he longed for vengeance, even if he himself should perish for it. He kept repeating prayers all night, but could get no peace. During the day he did not go near Makar Semyonich, nor even look at him.

A fortnight passed in this way. Aksionov could not sleep at night, and was so miserable that he did not know what to do.

One night as he was walking about the prison he noticed some earth that came rolling out from under one of the shelves on which the prisoners slept. He stopped to see what it was. Suddenly Makar Semyonich crept out from under the shelf, and looked up at Aksionov with frightened face. Aksionov tried to pass without looking at him, but Makar seized his hand and told him that he had dug a hole under the wall, getting rid of the earth by putting it into his high– boots, and emptying it out every day on the road when the prisoners were driven to their work.

"Just you keep quiet, old man, and you shall get out too. If you blab, they'll flog the life out of me, but I will kill you first."

Aksionov trembled with anger as he looked at his enemy. He drew his hand away, saying, "I have no wish to escape, and you have no need to kill me; you killed me long ago! As to telling of you– I may do so or not, as God shall direct."

Next day, when the convicts were led out to work, the convoy soldiers noticed that one or other of the prisoners emptied some earth out of his boots. The prison was searched and the tunnel found. The Governor came and questioned all the prisoners to find out who had dug the hole. They all denied any knowledge of it. Those who knew would not betray Makar Semyonich, knowing he would be flogged almost to death. At last the Governor turned to Aksionov whom he knew to be a just man, and said:

"You are a truthful old man; tell me, before God, who dug the hole?"

Makar Semyonich stood as if he were quite unconcerned, looking at the Governor and not so much as glancing at Aksionov. Aksionov's lips and hands trembled, and for a long time he could not utter a word. He thought, "Why should I screen him who ruined my life? Let him pay for what I have suffered. But if I tell, they will probably flog the life out of him, and maybe I suspect him wrongly. And, after all, what good would it be to me?"

"Well, old man," repeated the Governor, "tell me the truth: who has been digging under the wall?"

Aksionov glanced at Makar Semyonich, and said, "I cannot say, your honour. It is not God's will that I should tell! Do what you like with me; I am your hands."

However much the Governor! tried, Aksionov would say no more, and so the matter had to be left.

That night, when Aksionov was lying on his bed and just beginning to doze, some one came quietly and sat down on his bed. He peered through the darkness and recognised Makar.

"What more do you want of me?" asked Aksionov. "Why have you come here?"

Makar Semyonich was silent. So Aksionov sat up and said, "What do you want? Go away, or I will call the guard!"

Makar Semyonich bent close over Aksionov, and whispered, "Ivan Dmitrich, forgive me!"

"What for?" asked Aksionov.

"It was I who killed the merchant and hid the knife among your things. I meant to kill you too, but I heard a noise outside, so I hid the knife in your bag and escaped out of the window."

Aksionov was silent, and did not know what to say. Makar Semyonich slid off the bed– shelf and knelt upon the ground. "Ivan Dmitrich," said he, "forgive me! For the love of God, forgive me! I will confess that it was I who killed the merchant, and you will be released and can go to your home."

"It is easy for you to talk," said Aksionov, "but I have suffered for you these twenty– six years. Where could I go to now?... My wife is dead, and my children have forgotten me. I have nowhere to go..."

Makar Semyonich did not rise, but beat his head on the

floor. "Ivan Dmitrich, forgive me!" he cried. "When they flogged me with the knot it was not so hard to bear as it is to see you now ... yet you had pity on me, and did not tell. For Christ's sake forgive me, wretch that I am!" And he began to sob.

When Aksionov heard him sobbing he, too, began to weep. "God will forgive you!" said he. "Maybe I am a hundred times worse than you." And at these words his heart grew light, and the longing for home left him. He no longer had any desire to leave the prison, but only hoped for his last hour to come.

In spite of what Aksionov had said, Makar Semyonich confessed, his guilt. But when the order for his release came, Aksionov was already dead.

Papa Panov's Special Christmas

It was Christmas Eve and although it was still afternoon, lights had begun to appear in the shops and houses of the little Russian village, for the short winter day was nearly over. Excited children scurried indoors and now only muffled sounds of chatter and laughter escaped from closed shutters.

Old Papa Panov, the village shoemaker, stepped outside his shop to take one last look around. The sounds of happiness, the bright lights and the faint but delicious smells of Christmas cooking reminded him of past Christmas times when his wife had still been alive and his own children little. Now they had gone. His usually cheerful face, with the little laughter wrinkles behind the round steel spectacles, looked sad now. But he went back indoors with a firm step, put up the shutters and set a pot of coffee to heat on the charcoal stove. Then, with a sigh, he settled in his big armchair.

Papa Panov did not often read, but tonight he pulled down the big old family Bible and, slowly tracing the lines with one forefinger, he read again the Christmas story. He read how Mary and Joseph, tired by their journey to Bethlehem, found no room for them at the inn, so that Mary's little baby was born in the cowshed.

"Oh, dear, oh, dear!" exclaimed Papa Panov, "if only they had come here! I would have given them my bed and I could have covered the baby with my patchwork quilt to keep him warm."

He read on about the wise men who had come to see the baby Jesus, bringing him splendid gifts. Papa Panov's face fell. "I have no gift that I could give him," he thought sadly.

Then his face brightened. He put down the Bible, got up and stretched his long arms t the shelf high up in his little room. He took down a small, dusty box and opened it. Inside was a perfect pair of tiny leather shoes. Papa Panov smiled with satisfaction. Yes, they were as good as he had remembered – the best shoes he had ever made. "I should give him those," he decided, as he gently put them away and sat down again.

He was feeling tired now, and the further he read the sleepier he became. The print began to dance before his eyes so that he closed them, just for a minute. In no time at all Papa Panov was fast asleep.

And as he slept he dreamed. He dreamed that someone was in his room and he knew at once, as one does in dreams, who the person was. It was Jesus.

"You have been wishing that you could see me, Papa Panov." he said kindly, "then look for me tomorrow. It will be Christmas Day and I will visit you. But look carefully, for I shall not tell you who I am."

When at last Papa Panov awoke, the bells were ringing out and a thin light was filtering through the shutters. "Bless my soul!" said Papa Panov. "It's Christmas Day!"

He stood up and stretched himself for he was rather stiff. Then his face filled with happiness as he remembered his dream. This would be a very special Christmas after all, for Jesus was coming to visit him. How would he look? Would he be a little baby, as at that first Christmas? Would he be a grown man, a carpenter – or the great King that he is, God's Son? He must watch carefully the whole day through so that he recognized him however he came.

Papa Panov put on a special pot of coffee for his Christmas breakfast, took down the shutters and looked out of the window. The street was deserted, no one was stirring yet. No one except the road sweeper. He looked as miserable and dirty as ever, and well he might! Whoever wanted to work on Christmas Day – and in the raw cold and bitter freezing mist of such a morning?

Papa Panov opened the shop door, letting in a thin stream of cold air. "Come in!" he shouted across the street cheerily. "Come in and have some hot coffee to keep out the cold!"

The sweeper looked up, scarcely able to believe his ears. He was only too glad to put down his broom and come into the warm room. His old clothes steamed gently in the heat of the stove and he clasped both red hands round the comforting warm mug as he drank.

Papa Panov watched him with satisfaction, but every now and them his eyes strayed to the window. It would never do to miss his special visitor.

"Expecting someone?" the sweeper asked at last. So Papa Panov told him about his dream.

"Well, I hope he comes," the sweeper said, "you've given me a bit of Christmas cheer I never expected to have. I'd say you deserve to have your dream come true." And he actually smiled.

When he had gone, Papa Panov put on cabbage soup for his dinner, then went to the door again, scanning the street. He saw no one. But he was mistaken. Someone was coming.

The girl walked so slowly and quietly, hugging the walls of shops and houses, that it was a while before he noticed her. She looked very tired and she was carrying something. As she drew nearer he could see that it was a baby, wrapped in a thin shawl. There was such sadness in her face and in the pinched little face of the baby, that Papa Panov's heart went out to them.

"Won't you come in," he called, stepping outside to meet them. "You both need a warm seat by the fire and a rest."

The young mother let him shepherd her indoors and to the comfort of the armchair. She gave a big sigh of relief.

"I'll warm some milk for the baby," Papa Panov said, "I've had children of my own – I can feed her for you." He took the milk from the stove and carefully fed the baby from a spoon, warming her tiny feet by the stove at the same time.

"She needs shoes," the cobbler said.

But the girl replied, "I can't afford shoes, I've got no husband to bring home money. I'm on my way to the next village to get work."

A sudden thought flashed through Papa Panov's mind. He remembered the little shoes he had looked at last night. But he had been keeping those for Jesus. He looked again at the cold little feet and made up his mind.

"Try these on her," he said, handing the baby and the shoes to the mother. The beautiful little shoes were a perfect fit. The girl smiled happily and the baby gurgled with pleasure.

"You have been so kind to us," the girl said, when she got up with her baby to go. "May all your Christmas wishes come true!"

But Papa Panov was beginning to wonder if his very special Christmas wish would come true. Perhaps he had missed his visitor? He looked anxiously up and down the street. There were plenty of people about but they were all faces that he recognized. There were neighbors going to call on their families. They nodded and smiled and wished him Happy Christmas! Or beggars – and Papa Panov hurried indoors to fetch them hot soup and a generous hunk of bread, hurrying out again in case he missed the Important Stranger.

All too soon the winter dusk fell. When Papa Panov next went to the door and strained his eyes, he could no longer make out the passers– by. Most were home and indoors by now anyway. He walked slowly back into his room at last, put up the shutters, and sat down wearily in his armchair.

So it had been just a dream after all. Jesus had not come.

Then all at once he knew that he was no longer alone in the room.

This was not dream for he was wide awake. At first he seemed to see before his eyes the long stream of people who had come to him that day. He saw again the old road sweeper, the young mother and her baby and the beggars he had fed. As they passed, each whispered, "Didn't you see me, Papa Panov?"

"Who are you?" he called out, bewildered.

Then another voice answered him. It was the voice from his dream – the voice of Jesus.

"I was hungry and you fed me," he said. "I was naked and you clothed me. I was cold and you warmed me. I came to you today in everyone of those you helped and welcomed."

Then all was quiet and still. Only the sound of the big clock ticking. A great peace and happiness seemed to fill the room, overflowing Papa Panov's heart until he wanted to burst out singing and laughing and dancing with joy.

"So he did come after all!" was all that he said.

Three Questions

It once occurred to a certain king, that if he always knew the right time to begin everything; if he knew who were the right people to listen to, and whom to avoid; and, above all, if he always knew what was the most important thing to do, he would never fail in anything he might undertake.

And this thought having occurred to him, he had it proclaimed throughout his kingdom that he would give a great reward to any one who would teach him what was the right time for every action, and who were the most necessary people, and how he might know what was the most important thing to do.

And learned men came to the King, but they all answered his questions differently.

In reply to the first question, some said that to know the right time for every action, one must draw up in advance, a table of days, months and years, and must live strictly according to it. Only thus, said they, could everything be done at its proper time. Others declared that it was impossible to decide beforehand the right time for every action; but that, not letting oneself be absorbed in idle pastimes, one should always attend to all that was going on, and then do what was most needful. Others, again, said that however attentive the King might be to what was going on, it was impossible for one man to decide correctly the right time for every action, but that he should have a Council of wise men, who would help him to fix the proper time for everything.

But then again others said there were some things which could not wait to be laid before a Council, but about which one had at once to decide whether to undertake them or not. But in order to decide that, one must know beforehand what was going to happen. It is only magicians who know that; and, therefore, in order to know the right time for every action, one must consult magicians.

Equally various were the answers to the second question. Some said, the people the King most needed were his councillors; others, the priests; others, the doctors; while some said the warriors were the most necessary.

To the third question, as to what was the most important occupation: some replied that the most important thing in the world was science. Others said it was skill in warfare; and others, again, that it was religious worship.

All the answers being different, the King agreed with none of them, and gave the reward to none. But still wishing to find the right answers to his questions, he decided to consult a hermit, widely renowned for his wisdom.

The hermit lived in a wood which he never quitted, and he received none but common folk. So the King put on simple clothes, and before reaching the hermit's cell dismounted from his horse, and, leaving his body– guard behind, went on alone.

When the King approached, the hermit was digging the ground in front of his hut. Seeing the King, he greeted him and went on digging. The hermit was frail and weak, and each time he stuck his spade into the ground and turned a little earth, he breathed heavily.

The King went up to him and said: "I have come to you, wise hermit, to ask you to answer three questions: How can I learn to do the right thing at the right time? Who are the people I most need, and to whom should I, therefore, pay more attention than to the rest? And, what affairs are the most important, and need my first attention?"

The hermit listened to the King, but answered nothing. He just spat on his hand and recommenced digging.

"You are tired," said the King, "let me take the spade and work awhile for you."

"Thanks!" said the hermit, and, giving the spade to the King, he sat down on the ground.

When he had dug two beds, the King stopped and repeated his questions. The hermit again gave no answer, but rose, stretched out his hand for the spade, and said:

"Now rest awhile– and let me work a bit."

But the King did not give him the spade, and continued to dig. One hour passed, and another. The sun began to sink behind the trees, and the King at last stuck the spade into the ground, and said:

"I came to you, wise man, for an answer to my questions. If you can give me none, tell me so, and I will return home."

"Here comes some one running," said the hermit, "let us see who it is."

The King turned round, and saw a bearded man come running out of the wood. The man held his hands pressed against his stomach, and blood was flowing from under them. When he reached the King, he fell fainting on the ground moaning feebly. The King and the hermit unfastened the man's clothing. There was a large wound in his stomach. The King washed it as best he could, and bandaged it with his handkerchief and with a towel the hermit had. But the blood would not stop flowing, and the King again and again removed the bandage soaked with warm blood, and washed and rebandaged the wound. When at last the blood ceased flowing, the man revived and asked for something to drink. The King brought fresh water and gave it to him. Meanwhile the sun had set, and it had become cool. So the King, with the hermit's help, carried the wounded man into the hut and laid him on the bed. Lying on the bed the man closed his eyes and was quiet; but the King was so tired with his walk and with the work he had done, that he crouched down on the threshold, and also fell asleep— so soundly that he slept all through the short summer night. When he awoke in the morning, it was long before he could remember where he was, or who was the strange bearded man lying on the bed and gazing intently at him with shining eyes.

"Forgive me!" said the bearded man in a weak voice, when he saw that the King was awake and was looking at him.

"I do not know you, and have nothing to forgive you for," said the King.

"You do not know me, but I know you. I am that enemy of yours who swore to revenge himself on you, because you executed his brother and seized his property. I knew you had gone alone to see the hermit, and I resolved to kill you on your way back. But the day passed and you did not return. So I came out from my ambush to find you, and I came upon your bodyguard, and they recognized me, and wounded me. I escaped from them, but should have bled to death had you not dressed my wound. I wished to kill you, and you have saved my life. Now, if I live, and if you wish it, I will serve you as your most faithful slave, and will bid my sons do the same. Forgive me!"

The King was very glad to have made peace with his enemy so easily, and to have gained him for a friend, and he not only forgave him, but said he would send his servants and his own physician to attend him, and promised to restore his property.

Having taken leave of the wounded man, the King went out into the porch and looked around for the hermit. Before going away he wished once more to beg an answer to the questions he had put. The hermit was outside, on his knees, sowing seeds in the beds that had been dug the day before.

The King approached him, and said:

"For the last time, I pray you to answer my questions, wise man."

"You have already been answered!" said the hermit, still crouching on his thin legs, and looking up at the King, who stood before him.

"How answered? What do you mean?" asked the King.

"Do you not see," replied the hermit. "If you had not pitied my weakness yesterday, and had not dug those beds for me, but had gone your way, that man would have attacked you, and you would have repented of not having stayed with me. So the most important time was when you were digging the beds; and I was the most important man; and to do me good was your most important business. Afterwards when that man ran to us, the most important time was when you were attending to him, for if you had not bound up his wounds he would have died without having made peace with you. So he was the most important man, and what you did for him was your most important business. Remember then: there is only one time that is important—Now! It is the most important time because it is the only time when we have any power. The most necessary man is he with whom you are, for no man knows whether he will ever have dealings with any one else: and the most important affair is, to do him good, because for that purpose alone was man sent into this life!"

Work, Death and Sickness

A Legend

This is a legend current among the South American Indians. God, say they, at first made men so that they had no need to work: they needed neither houses, nor clothes, nor food, and they all lived till they were a hundred, and did not know what illness was.

When, after some time, God looked to see how people were living, he saw that instead of being happy in their life, they had quarrelled with one another, and, each caring for himself, had brought matters to such a pass that far from enjoying life, they cursed it.

Then God said to himself: 'This comes of their living separately, each for himself.' And to change this state of things, God so arranged matters that it became impossible for people to live without working. To avoid suffering from cold and hunger, they were now obliged to build dwellings, and to dig the ground, and to grow and gather fruits and grain.

'Work will bring them together,' thought God. 'They cannot make their tools, prepare and transport their timber, build their houses, sow and gather their harvests, spin and weave, and make their clothes, each one alone by himself.'

'It will make them understand that the more heartily they work together, the more they will have and the better they will live; and this will unite them.'

Time passed on, and again God came to see how men were living, and whether they were now happy.

But he found them living worse than before. They worked together (that they could not help doing), but not all together, being broken up into little groups. And each group tried to snatch work from other groups, and they hindered one another, wasting time and strength in their struggles, so that things went ill with them all.

Having seen that this, too, was not well, God decided so as to arrange things that man should not know the time of his death, but might die at any moment; and he announced this to them.

'Knowing that each of them may die at any moment,' thought God, 'they will not, by grasping at gains that may last so short a time, spoil the hours of life allotted to them.'

But it turned out otherwise. When God returned to see how people were living, he saw that their life was as bad as ever.

Those who were strongest, availing themselves of the fact that men might die at any time, subdued those who were weaker, killing some and threatening others with death. And it came about that the strongest and their descendants did no work, and suffered from the weariness of idleness, while those who were weaker had to work beyond their strength, and suffered from lack of rest. Each set of men feared and hated the other. And the life of man became yet more unhappy.

Having seen all this, God, to mend matters, decided to make use of one last means; he sent all kinds of sickness among men. God thought that when all men were exposed to sickness they would understand that those who are well should have pity on those who are sick, and should help them, that when they themselves fall ill those who are well might in turn help them.

And again God went away, but when He came back to see how men lived now that they were subject to sicknesses, he saw that their life was worse even than before. The very sickness that in God's purpose should have united men, had divided them more than ever. Those men who were strong enough to make others work, forced them also to wait on them in times of sickness; but they did not, in their turn, look after others who were ill. And those who were forced to work for others and to look after them when sick, were so worn with work that they had no time to look after their own sick, but left them without attendance. That the sight of sick folk might not disturb the pleasures of the wealthy, houses were arranged in which these poor people suffered and died, far from those whose sympathy might have cheered them, and in the arms of hired people who nursed them without compassion, or even with disgust. Moreover, people considered many of the illnesses infectious, and, fearing to catch them, not only avoided the sick, but even separated themselves from those who attended the sick.

Then God said to Himself: 'If even this means will not bring men to understand wherein their happiness lies, let them be taught by suffering.' And God left men to themselves.

And, left to themselves, men lived long before they understood that they all ought to, and might be, happy. Only in the very latest times have a few of them begun to understand that work ought not to be a bugbear to some and like galley– slavery for others, but should be a common and happy occupation, uniting all men. They have begun to understand that with death constantly threatening each of us, the only reasonable business of every man is to spend the years, months, hours, and minutes, allotted him–in unity and love. They have begun to understand that sickness, far from dividing men, should, on the contrary, give opportunity for loving union with one another.

How Much Land Does a Man Needs?

I

An elder sister came to visit her younger sister in the country. The elder was married to a tradesman in town, the younger to a peasant in the village. As the sisters sat over their tea talking, the elder began to boast of the advantages of town life: saying how comfortably they lived there, how well they dressed, what fine clothes her children wore, what good things they ate and drank, and how she went to the theatre, promenades, and entertainments.

The younger sister was piqued, and in turn disparaged the life of a tradesman, and stood up for that of a peasant.

"I would not change my way of life for yours," said she. "We may live roughly, but at least we are free from anxiety. You live in better style than we do, but though you often earn more than you need, you are very likely to lose all you have. You know the proverb, 'Loss and gain are brothers twain.' It often happens that people who are wealthy one day are begging their bread the next. Our way is safer. Though a peasant's life is not a fat one, it is a long one. We shall never grow rich, but we shall always have enough to eat."

The elder sister said sneeringly:

"Enough? Yes, if you like to share with the pigs and the calves! What do you know of elegance or manners! However much your good man may slave, you will die as you are living— on a dung heap— and your children the same."

"Well, what of that?" replied the younger. "Of course our work is rough and coarse. But, on the other hand, it is sure; and we need not bow to any one. But you, in your towns, are surrounded by temptations; today all may be right, but tomorrow the Evil One may tempt your husband with cards, wine, or women, and all will go to ruin. Don't such things happen often enough?"

Pahom, the master of the house, was lying on the top of the oven, and he listened to the women's chatter.

"It is perfectly true," thought he. "Busy as we are from childhood tilling Mother Earth, we peasants have no time to let any nonsense settle in our heads. Our only trouble is that we haven't land enough. If I had plenty of land, I shouldn't fear the Devil himself!"

The women finished their tea, chatted a while about dress, and then cleared away the tea– things and lay down to sleep.

But the Devil had been sitting behind the oven, and had heard all that was said. He was pleased that the peasant's wife had led her husband into boasting, and that he had said that if he had plenty of land he would not fear the Devil himself.

"All right," thought the Devil. "We will have a tussle. I'll give you land enough; and by means of that land I will get you into my power."

II

Close to the village there lived a lady, a small landowner, who had an estate of about three hundred acres. She had always lived on good terms with the peasants, until she engaged as her steward an old soldier, who took to burdening the people with fines. However careful Pahom tried to be, it happened again and again that now a horse of his got among the lady's oats, now a cow strayed into her garden, now his calves found their way into her meadows– and he always had to pay a fine.

Pahom paid, but grumbled, and, going home in a temper, was rough with his family. All through that summer Pahom had much trouble because of this steward; and he was even glad when winter came and the cattle had to be stabled. Though he grudged the fodder when they could no longer graze on the pasture– land, at least he was free from anxiety about them.

In the winter the news got about that the lady was going to sell her land, and that the keeper of the inn on the high road was bargaining for it. When the peasants heard this they were very much alarmed.

"Well," thought they, "if the innkeeper gets the land he will worry us with fines worse than the lady's steward. We all depend on that estate."

So the peasants went on behalf of their Commune, and asked the lady not to sell the land to the innkeeper; offering her a better price for it themselves. The lady agreed to let them have it. Then the peasants tried to arrange for the Commune to buy the whole estate, so that it might be held by all in common. They met twice to discuss it, but could not settle the matter; the Evil One sowed discord among them, and they could not agree. So they decided to buy the land individually, each according to his means; and the lady agreed to this plan as she had to the other.

Presently Pahom heard that a neighbor of his was buying fifty acres, and that the lady had consented to accept one half in cash and to wait a year for the other half. Pahom felt envious.

"Look at that," thought he, "the land is all being sold, and I shall get none of it." So he spoke to his wife.

"Other people are buying," said he, "and we must also buy twenty acres or so. Life is becoming impossible. That steward is simply crushing us with his fines."

So they put their heads together and considered how they could manage to buy it. They had one hundred roubles laid by. They sold a colt, and one half of their bees; hired out one of their sons as a laborer, and took his wages in advance; borrowed the rest from a brother– in– law, and so scraped together half the purchase money.

Having done this, Pahom chose out a farm of forty acres, some of it wooded, and went to the lady to bargain for it. They came to an agreement, and he shook hands with her upon it, and paid her a deposit in advance. Then they went to town and signed the deeds; he paying half the price down, and undertaking to pay the remainder within two years.

So now Pahom had land of his own. He borrowed seed, and sowed it on the land he had bought. The harvest was a good one, and within a year he had managed to pay off his debts both to the lady and to his brother– in– law. So he became a landowner, ploughing and sowing his own land, making hay on his own land, cutting his own trees, and feeding his cattle on his own pasture. When he went out to plough his fields, or to look at his growing corn, or at his grass meadows, his heart would fill with joy. The grass that grew and the flowers that bloomed there, seemed to him unlike any that grew elsewhere. Formerly, when he had passed by that land, it had appeared the same as any other land, but now it seemed quite different.

III

So Pahom was well contented, and everything would have been right if the neighboring peasants would only not have trespassed on his corn– fields and meadows. He appealed to them most civilly, but they still went on: now the Communal herdsmen would let the village cows stray into his meadows; then horses from the night pasture would get among his corn. Pahom turned them out again and again, and forgave their owners, and for a long time he forbore from prosecuting any one. But at last he lost patience and complained to the District Court. He knew it was the peasants' want of land, and no evil intent on their part, that caused the trouble; but he thought:

"I cannot go on overlooking it, or they will destroy all I have. They must be taught a lesson."

So he had them up, gave them one lesson, and then another, and two or three of the peasants were fined. After a time Pahom's neighbours began to bear him a grudge for this, and would now and then let their cattle on his land on purpose. One peasant even got into Pahom's wood at night and cut down five young lime trees for their bark. Pahom passing through the wood one day noticed something white. He came nearer, and saw the stripped trunks lying on the ground, and close by stood the stumps, where the tree had been. Pahom was furious.

"If he had only cut one here and there it would have been bad enough," thought Pahom, "but the rascal has actually cut down a whole clump. If I could only find out who did this, I would pay him out."

He racked his brains as to who it could be. Finally he decided: "It must be Simon– no one else could have done it." Se he went to Simon's homestead to have a look around, but he found nothing, and only had an angry scene. However' he now felt more certain than ever that Simon had done it, and he lodged a complaint. Simon was summoned. The case was tried, and re– tried, and at the end of it all Simon was acquitted, there being no evidence against him. Pahom felt still more aggrieved, and let his anger loose upon the Elder and the Judges.

"You let thieves grease your palms," said he. "If you were honest folk yourselves, you would not let a thief go free."

So Pahom quarrelled with the Judges and with his neighbors. Threats to burn his building began to be uttered. So though Pahom had more land, his place in the Commune was much worse than before.

About this time a rumor got about that many people were moving to new parts.

"There's no need for me to leave my land," thought Pahom. "But some of the others might leave our village, and then there would be more room for us. I would take over their land myself, and make my estate a bit bigger. I could then live more at ease. As it is, I am still too cramped to be comfortable."

One day Pahom was sitting at home, when a peasant passing through the village, happened to call in. He was allowed to stay the night, and supper was given him. Pahom had a talk with this peasant and asked him where he came from. The stranger answered that he came from beyond the Volga, where he had been working. One word led to another, and the man went on to say that many people were settling in those parts. He told how some people from his village had settled there. They had joined the Commune, and had had twenty– five acres per man granted them. The land was so good, he said, that the rye sown on it grew as high as a horse, and so thick that five cuts of a sickle made a sheaf. One peasant, he said, had brought nothing with him but his bare hands, and now he had six horses and two cows of his own.

Pahom's heart kindled with desire. He thought:

"Why should I suffer in this narrow hole, if one can live so well elsewhere? I will sell my land and my homestead here, and with the money I will start afresh over there and get everything new. In this crowded place one is always having trouble. But I must first go and find out all about it myself."

Towards summer he got ready and started. He went down the Volga on a steamer to Samara, then walked another three hundred miles on foot, and at last reached the place. It was just as the stranger had said. The peasants had plenty of land: every man had twenty– five acres of Communal land given him for his use, and any one who had money could buy, besides, at fifty– cents an acre as much good freehold land as he wanted.

Having found out all he wished to know, Pahom returned home as autumn came on, and began selling off his belongings. He sold his land at a profit, sold his homestead and all his cattle, and withdrew from membership of the Commune. He only waited till the spring, and then started with his family for the new settlement.

IV

As soon as Pahom and his family arrived at their new abode, he applied for admission into the Commune of a large village. He stood treat to the Elders, and obtained the necessary documents. Five shares of Communal land were given him for his own and his sons' use: that is to say– 125 acres (not altogether, but in different fields) besides the use of the Communal pasture. Pahom put up the buildings he needed, and bought cattle. Of the Communal land alone he had three times as much as at his former home, and the land was good corn– land. He was ten times better off than he had been. He had plenty of arable land and pasturage, and could keep as many head of cattle as he liked.

At first, in the bustle of building and settling down, Pahom was pleased with it all, but when he got used to it he began to think that even here he had not enough land. The first year, he sowed wheat on his share of the Communal land, and had a good crop. He wanted to go on sowing wheat, but had not enough Communal land for the purpose, and what he had already used was not available; for in those parts wheat is only sown on virgin soil or on fallow land. It is sown for one or two years, and then the land lies fallow till it is again overgrown with prairie grass. There were many who wanted such land, and there was not enough for all; so that people quarrelled about it. Those who were better off, wanted it for growing wheat, and those who were poor, wanted it to let to dealers, so that they might raise money to pay their taxes. Pahom wanted to sow more wheat; so he rented land from a dealer for a year. He sowed much wheat and had a fine crop, but the land was too far from the village– the wheat had to be carted more than ten miles. After a time Pahom noticed that some peasant– dealers were living on separate farms, and were growing wealthy; and he thought:

"If I were to buy some freehold land, and have a homestead on it, it would be a different thing, altogether. Then it would all be nice and compact."

The question of buying freehold land recurred to him again and again.

He went on in the same way for three years; renting land and sowing wheat. The seasons turned out well and the crops were good, so that he began to lay money by. He might have gone on living contentedly, but he grew tired of having to rent other people's land every year, and having to scramble for it. Wherever there was good land to be had, the peasants would rush for it and it was taken up at once, so that unless you were sharp about it you got none. It happened in the third year that he and a dealer together rented a piece of pasture land from some peasants; and they had already ploughed it up, when there was some dispute, and the peasants went to law about it, and things fell out so that the labor was all lost. "If it were my own land," thought Pahom, "I should be independent, and there would not be all this unpleasantness."

So Pahom began looking out for land which he could buy; and he came across a peasant who had bought thirteen hundred acres, but having got into difficulties was willing to sell again cheap. Pahom bargained and haggled with him, and at last they settled the price at 1,500 roubles, part in cash and part to be paid later. They had all but clinched the matter, when a passing dealer happened to stop at Pahom's one day to get a feed for his horse. He drank tea with Pahom, and they had a talk. The dealer said that he was just returning from the land of the Bashkirs, far away, where he had bought thirteen thousand acres of land all for 1,000 roubles. Pahom questioned him further, and the tradesman said:

"All one need do is to make friends with the chiefs. I gave away about one hundred roubles' worth of dressing– gowns and carpets, besides a case of tea, and I gave wine to those who would drink it; and I got the land for less than two cents an acre. And he showed Pahom the title– deeds, saying:

"The land lies near a river, and the whole prairie is virgin soil."

Pahom plied him with questions, and the tradesman said:

"There is more land there than you could cover if you walked a year, and it all belongs to the Bashkirs. They are as simple as sheep, and land can be got almost for nothing."

"There now," thought Pahom, "with my one thousand roubles, why should I get only thirteen hundred acres, and saddle myself with a debt besides. If I take it out there, I can get more than ten times as much for the money."

V

Pahom inquired how to get to the place, and as soon as the tradesman had left him, he prepared to go there himself. He left his wife to look after the homestead, and started on his journey taking his man with him. They stopped at a town on their way, and bought a case of tea, some wine, and other presents, as the tradesman had advised. On and on they went until they had gone more than three hundred miles, and on the seventh day they came to a place where the Bashkirs had pitched their tents. It was all just as the tradesman had said. The people lived on the steppes, by a river, in felt– covered tents. They neither tilled the ground, nor ate bread. Their cattle and horses grazed in herds on the steppe. The colts were tethered behind the tents, and the mares were driven to them twice a day. The mares were milked, and from the milk kumiss was made. It was the women who prepared kumiss, and they also made cheese. As far as the men were concerned, drinking kumiss and tea, eating mutton, and playing on their pipes, was all they cared about. They were all stout and merry, and all the summer long they never thought of doing any work. They were quite ignorant, and knew no Russian, but were good– natured enough.

As soon as they saw Pahom, they came out of their tents and gathered round their visitor. An interpreter was found, and Pahom told them he had come about some land. The Bashkirs seemed very glad; they took Pahom and led him into one of the best tents, where they made him sit on some down cushions placed on a carpet, while they sat round him. They gave him tea and kumiss, and had a sheep killed, and gave him mutton to eat. Pahom took presents out of his cart and distributed them among the Bashkirs, and divided amongst them the tea. The Bashkirs were delighted. They talked a great deal among themselves, and then told the interpreter to translate.

"They wish to tell you," said the interpreter, "that they like you, and that it is our custom to do all we can to please a guest and to repay him for his gifts. You have given us presents, now tell us which of the things we possess please you best, that we may present them to you."

"What pleases me best here," answered Pahom, "is your land. Our land is crowded, and the soil is exhausted; but you have plenty of land and it is good land. I never saw the like of it."

The interpreter translated. The Bashkirs talked among themselves for a while. Pahom could not understand what they were saying, but saw that they were much amused, and that they shouted and laughed. Then they were silent and looked at Pahom while the interpreter said:

"They wish me to tell you that in return for your presents they will gladly give you as much land as you want. You have only to point it out with your hand and it is yours."

The Bashkirs talked again for a while and began to dispute. Pahom asked what they were disputing about, and the interpreter told him that some of them thought they ought to ask their Chief about the land and not act in his absence, while others thought there was no need to wait for his return.

VI

While the Bashkirs were disputing, a man in a large fox-fur cap appeared on the scene. They all became silent and rose to their feet. The interpreter said, "This is our Chief himself."

Pahom immediately fetched the best dressing-gown and five pounds of tea, and offered these to the Chief. The Chief accepted them, and seated himself in the place of honour. The Bashkirs at once began telling him something. The Chief listened for a while, then made a sign with his head for them to be silent, and addressing himself to Pahom, said in Russian:

"Well, let it be so. Choose whatever piece of land you like; we have plenty of it."

"How can I take as much as I like?" thought Pahom. "I must get a deed to make it secure, or else they may say, 'It is yours,' and afterwards may take it away again."

"Thank you for your kind words," he said aloud. "You have much land, and I only want a little. But I should like to be sure which bit is mine. Could it not be measured and made over to me? Life and death are in God's hands. You good people give it to me, but your children might wish to take it away again."

"You are quite right," said the Chief. "We will make it over to you."

"I heard that a dealer had been here," continued Pahom, "and that you gave him a little land, too, and signed title-deeds to that effect. I should like to have it done in the same way."

The Chief understood.

"Yes," replied he, "that can be done quite easily. We have a scribe, and we will go to town with you and have the deed properly sealed."

"And what will be the price?" asked Pahom.

"Our price is always the same: one thousand roubles a day."

Pahom did not understand.

"A day? What measure is that? How many acres would that be?"

"We do not know how to reckon it out," said the Chief. "We sell it by the day. As much as you can go round on your feet in a day is yours, and the price is one thousand roubles a day."

Pahom was surprised.

"But in a day you can get round a large tract of land," he said.

The Chief laughed.

"It will all be yours!" said he. "But there is one condition: If you don't return on the same day to the spot whence you started, your money is lost."

"But how am I to mark the way that I have gone?"

"Why, we shall go to any spot you like, and stay there. You must start from that spot and make your round, taking a spade with you. Wherever you think necessary, make a mark. At every turning, dig a hole and pile up the turf; then afterwards we will go round with a plough from hole to hole. You may make as large a circuit as you please, but before the sun sets you must return to the place you started from. All the land you cover will be yours."

Pahom was delighted. It– was decided to start early next morning. They talked a while, and after drinking some more kumiss and eating some more mutton, they had tea again, and then the night came on. They gave Pahom a feather– bed to sleep on, and the Bashkirs dispersed for the night, promising to assemble the next morning at daybreak and ride out before sunrise to the appointed spot.

VII

Pahom lay on the feather– bed, but could not sleep. He kept thinking about the land.

"What a large tract I will mark off!" thought he. "I can easily go thirty– five miles in a day. The days are long now, and within a circuit of thirty– five miles what a lot of land there will be! I will sell the poorer land, or let it to peasants, but I'll pick out the best and farm it. I will buy two ox– teams, and hire two more laborers. About a hundred and fifty acres shall be plough– land, and I will pasture cattle on the rest."

Pahom lay awake all night, and dozed off only just before dawn. Hardly were his eyes closed when he had a dream. He thought he was lying in that same tent, and heard somebody chuckling outside. He wondered who it could be, and rose and went out, and he saw the Bashkir Chief sitting in front of the tent holding his side and rolling about with laughter. Going nearer to the Chief, Pahom asked: "What are you laughing at?" But he saw that it was no longer the Chief, but the dealer who had recently stopped at his house and had told him about the land. Just as Pahom was going to ask, "Have you been here long?" he saw that it was not the dealer, but the peasant who had come up from the Volga, long ago, to Pahom's old home. Then he saw that it was not the peasant either, but the Devil himself with hoofs and horns, sitting there and chuckling, and before him lay a man barefoot, prostrate on the ground, with only trousers and a shirt on. And Pahom dreamt that he looked more attentively to see what sort of a man it was lying there, and he saw that the man was dead, and that it was himself! He awoke horror– struck.

"What things one does dream," thought he.

Looking round he saw through the open door that the dawn was breaking.

"It's time to wake them up," thought he. "We ought to be starting."

He got up, roused his man (who was sleeping in his cart), bade him harness; and went to call the Bashkirs.

"It's time to go to the steppe to measure the land," he said.

The Bashkirs rose and assembled, and the Chief came, too. Then they began drinking kumiss again, and offered Pahom some tea, but he would not wait.

"If we are to go, let us go. It is high time," said he.

VIII

The Bashkirs got ready and they all started: some mounted on horses, and some in carts. Pahom drove in his own small cart with his servant, and took a spade with him. When they reached the steppe, the morning red was beginning to kindle. They ascended a hillock (called by the Bashkirs a shikhan) and dismounting from their carts and their horses, gathered in one spot. The Chief came up to Pahom and stretched out his arm towards the plain:

"See," said he, "all this, as far as your eye can reach, is ours. You may have any part of it you like."

Pahom's eyes glistened: it was all virgin soil, as flat as the palm of your hand, as black as the seed of a poppy, and in the hollows different kinds of grasses grew breast high.

The Chief took off his fox– fur cap, placed it on the ground and said:

"This will be the mark. Start from here, and return here again. All the land you go round shall be yours."

Pahom took out his money and put it on the cap. Then he took off his outer coat, remaining in his sleeveless under coat. He unfastened his girdle and tied it tight below his stomach, put a little bag of bread into the breast of his coat, and tying a flask of water to his girdle, he drew up the tops of his boots, took the spade from his man, and stood ready to start. He considered for some moments which way he had better go– it was tempting everywhere.

"No matter," he concluded, "I will go towards the rising sun."

He turned his face to the east, stretched himself, and waited for the sun to appear above the rim.

"I must lose no time," he thought, "and it is easier walking while it is still cool."

The sun's rays had hardly flashed above the horizon, before Pahom, carrying the spade over his shoulder, went down into the steppe.

Pahom started walking neither slowly nor quickly. After having gone a thousand yards he stopped, dug a hole and placed pieces of turf one on another to make it more visible. Then he went on; and now that he had walked off his stiffness he quickened his pace. After a while he dug another hole.

Pahom looked back. The hillock could be distinctly seen in the sunlight, with the people on it, and the glittering tires of the cartwheels. At a rough guess Pahom concluded that he had walked three miles. It was growing warmer; he took off his under– coat, flung it across his shoulder, and went on again. It had grown quite warm now; he looked at the sun, it was time to think of breakfast.

"The first shift is done, but there are four in a day, and it is too soon yet to turn. But I will just take off my boots," said he to himself.

He sat down, took off his boots, stuck them into his girdle, and went on. It was easy walking now.

"I will go on for another three miles," thought he, "and then turn to the left. The spot is so fine, that it would be a pity to lose it. The further one goes, the better the land seems."

He went straight on a for a while, and when he looked round, the hillock was scarcely visible and the people on it looked like black ants, and he could just see something glistening there in the sun.

"Ah," thought Pahom, "I have gone far enough in this direction, it is time to turn. Besides I am in a regular sweat, and very thirsty."

He stopped, dug a large hole, and heaped up pieces of turf. Next he untied his flask, had a drink, and then turned sharply to the left. He went on and on; the grass was high, and it was very hot.

Pahom began to grow tired: he looked at the sun and saw that it was noon.

"Well," he thought, "I must have a rest."

He sat down, and ate some bread and drank some water; but he did not lie down, thinking that if he did he might fall asleep. After sitting a little while, he went on again. At first he walked easily: the food had strengthened him; but it had become terribly hot, and he felt sleepy; still he went on, thinking: "An hour to suffer, a life– time to live."

He went a long way in this direction also, and was about to turn to the left again, when he perceived a damp hollow: "It would be a pity to leave that out," he thought. "Flax would do well there." So he went on past the hollow, and dug a hole on the other side of it before he turned the corner. Pahom looked towards the hillock. The heat made the air hazy: it seemed to be quivering, and through the haze the people on the hillock could scarcely be seen.

"Ah!" thought Pahom, "I have made the sides too long; I must make this one shorter." And he went along the third side, stepping faster. He looked at the sun: it was nearly half way to the horizon, and he had not yet done two miles of the third side of the square. He was still ten miles from the goal.

"No," he thought, "though it will make my land lopsided, I must hurry back in a straight line now. I might go too far, and as it is I have a great deal of land."

So Pahom hurriedly dug a hole, and turned straight towards the hillock.

IX

Pahom went straight towards the hillock, but he now walked with difficulty. He was done up with the heat, his bare feet were cut and bruised, and his legs began to fail. He longed to rest, but it was impossible if he meant to get back before sunset. The sun waits for no man, and it was sinking lower and lower.

"Oh dear," he thought, "if only I have not blundered trying for too much! What if I am too late?"

He looked towards the hillock and at the sun. He was still far from his goal, and the sun was already near the rim. Pahom walked on and on; it was very hard walking, but he went quicker and quicker. He pressed on, but was still far from the place. He began running, threw away his coat, his boots, his flask, and his cap, and kept only the spade which he used as a support.

"What shall I do," he thought again, "I have grasped too much, and ruined the whole affair. I can't get there before the sun sets."

And this fear made him still more breathless. Pahom went on running, his soaking shirt and trousers stuck to him, and his mouth was parched. His breast was working like a blacksmith's bellows, his heart was beating like a hammer, and his legs were giving way as if they did not belong to him. Pahom was seized with terror lest he should die of the strain.

Though afraid of death, he could not stop. "After having run all that way they will call me a fool if I stop now," thought he. And he ran on and on, and drew near and heard the Bashkirs yelling and shouting to him, and their cries inflamed his heart still more. He gathered his last strength and ran on.

The sun was close to the rim, and cloaked in mist looked large, and red as blood. Now, yes now, it was about to set! The sun was quite low, but he was also quite near his aim. Pahom could already see the people on the hillock waving their arms to hurry him up. He could see the fox– fur cap on the ground, and the money on it, and the Chief sitting on the ground holding his sides. And Pahom remembered his dream.

"There is plenty of land," thought he, "but will God let me live on it? I have lost my life, I have lost my life! I shall never reach that spot!"

Pahom looked at the sun, which had reached the earth: one side of it had already disappeared. With all his remaining strength he rushed on, bending his body forward so that his legs could hardly follow fast enough to keep him from falling. Just as he reached the hillock it suddenly grew dark. He looked up– the sun had already set. He gave a cry: "All my labor has been in vain," thought he, and was about to stop, but he heard the Bashkirs still shouting, and remembered that though to him, from below, the sun seemed to have set, they on the hillock could still see it. He took a long breath and ran up the hillock. It was still light there. He reached the top and saw the cap. Before it sat the Chief laughing and holding his sides. Again Pahom remembered his dream, and he uttered a cry: his legs gave way beneath him, he fell forward and reached the cap with his hands.

"Ah, what a fine fellow!" exclaimed the Chief. "He has gained much land!"

Pahom's servant came running up and tried to raise him, but he saw that blood was flowing from his mouth. Pahom was dead!

The Bashkirs clicked their tongues to show their pity.

His servant picked up the spade and dug a grave long enough for Pahom to lie in, and buried him in it. Six feet from his head to his heels was all he needed.

The Death of Ivan Ilyich

Chapter I

During an interval in the Melvinski trial in the large building of the Law Courts the members and public prosecutor met in Ivan Egorovich Shebek's private room, where the conversation turned on the celebrated Krasovski case. Fedor Vasilievich warmly maintained that it was not subject to their jurisdiction, Ivan Egorovich maintained the contrary, while Peter Ivanovich, not having entered into the discussion at the start, took no part in it but looked through the Gazette which had just been handed in.

"Gentlemen," he said, "Ivan Ilych has died!"

"You don't say so!"

"Here, read it yourself," replied Peter Ivanovich, handing Fedor Vasilievich the paper still damp from the press. Surrounded by a black border were the words: "Praskovya Fedorovna Golovina, with profound sorrow, informs relatives and friends of the demise of her beloved husband Ivan Ilych Golovin, Member of the Court of Justice, which occurred on February the 4th of this year 1882. The funeral will take place on Friday at one o'clock in the afternoon."

Ivan Ilych had been a colleague of the gentlemen present and was liked by them all. He had been ill for some weeks with an illness said to be incurable. His post had been kept open for him, but there had been conjectures that in case of his death Alexeev might receive his appointment, and that either Vinnikov or Shtabel would succeed Alexeev. So on receiving the news of Ivan Ilych's death the first thought of each of the gentlemen in that private room was of the changes and promotions it might occasion among themselves or their acquaintances.

"I shall be sure to get Shtabel's place or Vinnikov's," thought Fedor Vasilievich. "I was promised that long ago, and the promotion means an extra eight hundred rubles a year for me besides the allowance."

"Now I must apply for my brother– in– law's transfer from Kaluga," thought Peter Ivanovich. "My wife will be very glad, and then she won't be able to say that I never do anything for her relations."

"I thought he would never leave his bed again," said Peter Ivanovich aloud. "It's very sad."

"But what really was the matter with him?"

"The doctors couldn't say – at least they could, but each of them said something different. When last I saw him I though he was getting better."

"And I haven't been to see him since the holidays. I always meant to go."

"Had he any property?"

"I think his wife had a little – but something quiet trifling."

"We shall have to go to see her, but they live so terribly far away."

"Far away from you, you mean. Everything's far away from your place."

"You see, he never can forgive my living on the other side of the river," said Peter Ivanovich, smiling at Shebek. Then, still talking of the distances between different parts of the city, they returned to the Court.

Besides considerations as to the possible transfers and promotions likely to result from Ivan Ilych's death, the mere fact of the death of a near acquaintance aroused, as usual, in all who heard of it the complacent feeling that, "it is he who is dead and not I."

Each one thought or felt, "Well, he's dead but I'm alive!" But the more intimate of Ivan Ilych's acquaintances, his so – called friends, could not help thinking also that they would now have to fulfil the very tiresome demands of propriety by attending the funeral service and paying a visit of condolence to the widow.

Fedor Vasilievich and Peter Ivanovich had been his nearest acquaintances. Peter Ivanovich had studied law with Ivan Ilych and had considered himself to be under obligations to him.

Having told his wife at dinner– time of Ivan Ilych's death, and of his conjecture that it might be possible to get her brother transferred to their circuit, Peter Ivanovich sacrificed his usual nap, put on his evening clothes and drove to Ivan Ilych's house.

At the entrance stood a carriage and two cabs. Leaning against the wall in the hall downstairs near the cloakstand was a coffin– lid covered with cloth of gold, ornamented with gold cord and tassels, that had been polished up with metal powder. Two ladies in black were taking off their fur cloaks. Peter Ivanovich recognized one of them as Ivan Ilych's sister, but the other was a stranger to him. His colleague Schwartz was just coming downstairs, but on seeing Peter Ivanovich enter he stopped and winked at him, as if to say: "Ivan Ilych has made a mess of things – not like you and me."

Schwartz's face with his Piccadilly whiskers, and his slim figure in evening dress, had as usual an air of elegant solemnity which contrasted with the playfulness of his character and had a special piquancy here, or so it seemed to Peter Ivanovich.

Peter Ivanovich allowed the ladies to precede him and slowly followed them upstairs. Schwartz did not come down but remained where he was, and Peter Ivanovich understood that he wanted to arrange where they should play bridge that evening. The ladies went upstairs to the widow's room, and Schwartz with seriously compressed lips but a playful looking his eyes, indicated by a twist of his eyebrows the room to the right where the body lay.

Peter Ivanovich, like everyone else on such occasions, entered feeling uncertain what he would have to do. All he knew was that at such times it is always safe to cross oneself. But he was not quite sure whether one should make obseisances while doing so. He therefore adopted a middle course. On entering the room he began crossing himself and made a slight movement resembling a bow. At the same time, as far as the motion of his head and arm allowed, he surveyed the room. Two young men – apparently nephews, one of whom was a high– school pupil – were leaving the room, crossing themselves as they did so. An old woman was standing motionless, and a lady with strangely arched eyebrows was saying something to her in a whisper. A vigorous, resolute Church Reader, in a frock– coat, was reading something in a loud voice with an expression that precluded any contradiction. The butler's assistant, Gerasim, stepping lightly in front of Peter Ivanovich, was strewing something on the floor. Noticing this, Peter Ivanovich was immediately aware of a faint odour of a decomposing body.

The last time he had called on Ivan Ilych, Peter Ivanovich had seen Gerasim in the study. Ivan Ilych had been particularly fond of him and he was performing the duty of a sick nurse.

Peter Ivanovich continued to make the sign of the cross slightly inclining his head in an intermediate direction between the coffin, the Reader, and the icons on the table in a corner of the room. Afterwards, when it seemed to him that this movement of his arm in crossing himself had gone on too long, he stopped and began to look at the corpse.

The dead man lay, as dead men always lie, in a specially heavy way, his rigid limbs sunk in the soft cushions of the coffin, with the head forever bowed on the pillow. His yellow waxen brow with bald patches over his sunken temples was thrust up in the way peculiar to the dead, the protruding nose seeming to press on the upper lip. He was much changed and grown even thinner since Peter Ivanovich had last seen him, but, as is always the case with the dead, his face was handsomer and above all more dignified than when he was alive. the expression on the face said that what was necessary had been accomplished, and accomplished rightly. Besides this there was in that expression a reproach and a warning to the living. This warning seemed to Peter Ivanovich out of place, or at least not applicable to him. He felt a certain discomfort and so he hurriedly crossed himself once more and turned and went out of the door – too hurriedly and too regardless of propriety, as he himself was aware.

Schwartz was waiting for him in the adjoining room with legs spread wide apart and both hands toying with his top-hat behind his back. The mere sight of that playful, well-groomed, and elegant figure refreshed Peter Ivanovich. He felt that Schwartz was above all these happenings and would not surrender to any depressing influences. His very look said that this incident of a church service for Ivan Ilych could not be a sufficient reason for infringing the order of the session – in other words, that it would certainly not prevent his unwrapping a new pack of cards and shuffling them that evening while a footman placed fresh candles on the table: in fact, that there was no reason for supposing that this incident would hinder their spending the evening agreeably.

Indeed he said this in a whisper as Peter Ivanovich passed him, proposing that they should meet for a game at Fedor Vasilievich's. But apparently Peter Ivanovich was not destined to play bridge that evening. Praskovya Fedorovna (a short, fat woman who despite all efforts to the contrary had continued to broaden steadily from her shoulders downwards and who had the same extraordinarily arched eyebrows as the lady who had been standing by the coffin), dressed all in black, her head covered with lace, came out of her own room with some other ladies, conducted them to the room where the dead body lay, and said: "The service will begin immediately. Please go in."

Schwartz, making an indefinite bow, stood still, evidently neither accepting nor declining this invitation. Praskovya Fedorovna recognizing Peter Ivanovich, sighed, went close up to him, took his hand, and said: "I know you were a true friend to Ivan Ilych..." and looked at him awaiting some suitable response. And Peter Ivanovich knew that, just as it had been the right thing to cross himself in that room, so what he had to do here was to press her hand, sigh, and say, "Believe me..." So he did all this and as he did it felt that the desired result had been achieved: that both he and she were touched.

"Come with me. I want to speak to you before it begins," said the widow. "Give me your arm."

Peter Ivanovich gave her his arm and they went to the inner rooms, passing Schwartz who winked at Peter Ivanovich compassionately.

"That does for our bridge! Don's object if we find another player. Perhaps you can cut in when you do escape," said his playful look.

Peter Ivanovich sighed still more deeply and despondently, and Praskovya Fedorovna pressed his arm gratefully. When they reached the drawing– room, upholstered in pink cretonne and lighted by a dim lamp, they sat down at the table – she on a sofa and Peter Ivanovich on a low pouffe, the springs of which yielded spasmodically under his weight. Praskovya Fedorovna had been on the point of warning him to take another seat, but felt that such a warning was out of keeping with her present condition and so changed her mind. As he sat down on the pouffe Peter Ivanovich recalled how Ivan Ilych had arranged this room and had consulted him regarding this pink cretonne with green leaves. The whole room was full of furniture and knick– knacks, and on her way to the sofa the lace of the widow's black shawl caught on the edge of the table. Peter Ivanovich rose to detach it, and the springs of the pouffe, relieved of his weight, rose also and gave him a push. The widow began detaching her shawl herself, and Peter Ivanovich again sat down, suppressing the rebellious springs of the pouffe under him. But the widow had not quite freed herself and Peter Ivanovich got up again, and again the pouffe rebelled and even creaked. When this was all over she took out a clean cambric handkerchief and began to weep. The episode with the shawl and the struggle with the pouffe had cooled Peter Ivanovich's emotions and he sat there with a sullen look on his face. This awkward situation was interrupted by Sokolov, Ivan Ilych's butler, who came to report that the plot in the cemetery that Praskovya Fedorovna had chosen would cost tow hundred rubles. She stopped weeping and, looking at Peter Ivanovich with the air of a victim, remarked in French that it was very hard for her. Peter Ivanovich made a silent gesture signifying his full conviction that it must indeed be so.

"Please smoke," she said in a magnanimous yet crushed voice, and turned to discuss with Sokolov the price of the plot for the grave.

Peter Ivanovich while lighting his cigarette heard her inquiring very circumstantially into the prices of different plots in the cemetery and finally decide which she would take. when that was done she gave instructions about engaging the choir. Sokolov then left the room.

"I look after everything myself," she told Peter Ivanovich, shifting the albums that lay on the table; and noticing that the table was endangered by his cigarette– ash, she immediately passed him an ash– tray, saying as she did so: "I consider it an affectation to say that my grief prevents my attending to practical affairs. On the contrary, if anything can – I won't say console me, but – distract me, it is seeing to everything concerning him." She again took out her handkerchief as if preparing to cry, but suddenly, as if mastering her feeling, she shook herself and began to speak calmly. "But there is something I want to talk to you about."

Peter Ivanovich bowed, keeping control of the springs of the pouffe, which immediately began quivering under him.

"He suffered terribly the last few days."

"Did he?" said Peter Ivanovich.

"Oh, terribly! He screamed unceasingly, not for minutes but for hours. for the last three days he screamed incessantly. It was unendurable. I cannot understand how I bore it; you could hear him three rooms off. Oh, what I have suffered!"

"Is it possible that he was conscious all that time?" asked Peter Ivanovich.

"Yes," she whispered. "To the last moment. He took leave of us a quarter of an hour before he died, and asked us to take Volodya away."

The thought of the suffering of this man he had known so intimately, first as a merry little boy, then as a schoolmate, and later as a grown– up colleague, suddenly struck Peter Ivanovich with horror, despite an unpleasant consciousness of his own and this woman's dissimulation. He again saw that brow, and that nose pressing down on the lip, and felt afraid for himself.

"Three days of frightful suffering and the death! Why, that might suddenly, at any time, happen to me," he thought, and for a moment felt terrified. But – he did not himself know how – the customary reflection at once occurred to him that this had happened to Ivan Ilych and not to him, and that it should not and could not happen to him, and that to think that it could would be yielding to depressing which he ought not to do, as Schwartz's expression plainly showed. After which reflection Peter Ivanovich felt reassured, and began to ask with interest about the details of Ivan Ilych's death, as though death was an accident natural to Ivan Ilych but certainly not to himself.

After many details of the really dreadful physical sufferings Ivan Ilych had endured (which details he learnt only from the effect those sufferings had produced on Praskovya Fedorovna's nerves) the widow apparently found it necessary to get to business.

"Oh, Peter Ivanovich, how hard it is! How terribly, terribly hard!" and she again began to weep.

Peter Ivanovich sighed and waited for her to finish blowing her nose. When she had don so he said, "Believe me..." and she again began talking and brought out what was evidently her chief concern with him – namely, to question him as to how she could obtain a grant of money from the government on the occasion of her husband's death. She made it appear that she was asking Peter Ivanovich's advice about her pension, but he soon saw that she already knew about that to the minutest detail, more even than he did himself. She knew how much could be got out of the government in consequence of her husband's death, but wanted to find out whether she could not possibly extract something more. Peter Ivanovich tried to think of some means of doing so, but after reflecting for a while and, out of propriety, condemning the government for its niggardliness, he said he thought that nothing more could be got. Then she sighed and evidently began to devise means of getting rid of her visitor. Noticing this, he put out his cigarette, rose, pressed her hand, and went out into the anteroom.

In the dining– room where the clock stood that Ivan Ilych had liked so much and had bought at an antique shop, Peter Ivanovich met a priest and a few acquaintances who had come to attend the service, and he recognized Ivan Ilych's daughter, a handsome young woman. She was in black and her slim figure appeared slimmer than ever. She had a gloomy, determined, almost angry expression, and bowed to Peter Ivanovich as though he were in some way to blame.

Behind her, with the same offended look, stood a wealthy young man, and examining magistrate, whom Peter Ivanovich also knew and who was her fiance, as he had heard. He bowed mournfully to them and was about to pass into the death– chamber, when from under the stairs appeared the figure of Ivan Ilych's schoolboy son, who was extremely like his father. He seemed a little Ivan Ilych, such as Peter Ivanovich remembered when they studied law together. His tear– stained eyes had in them the look that is seen in the eyes of boys of thirteen or fourteen who are not pure– minded. When he saw Peter Ivanovich he scowled morosely and shamefacedly. Peter Ivanovich nodded to him and entered the death– chamber. The service began: candles, groans, incense, tears, and sobs. Peter Ivanovich stood looking gloomily down at his feet. He did not look once at the dead man, did not yield to any depressing influence, and was one of the first to leave the room. There was no one in the anteroom, but Gerasim darted out of the dead man's room, rummaged with his strong hands among the fur coats to find Peter Ivanovich's and helped him on with it.

"Well, friend Gerasim," said Peter Ivanovich, so as to say something. "It's a sad affair, isn't it?"

"It's God will. We shall all come to it some day," said Gerasim, displaying his teeth – the even white teeth of a healthy peasant – and, like a man in the thick of urgent work, he briskly opened the front door, called the coachman, helped Peter Ivanovich into the sledge, and sprang back to the porch as if in readiness for what he had to do next.

Peter Ivanovich found the fresh air particularly pleasant after the smell of incense, the dead body, and carbolic acid.

"Where to sir?" asked the coachman.

"It's not too late even now....I'll call round on Fedor Vasilievich."

He accordingly drove there and found them just finishing the first rubber, so that it was quite convenient for him to cut in.

Chapter II

Ivan Ilych's life had been most simple and most ordinary and therefore most terrible.

He had been a member of the Court of Justice, and died at the age of forty– five. His father had been an official who after serving in various ministries and departments in Petersburg had made the sort of career which brings men to positions from which by reason of their long service they cannot be dismissed, though they are obviously unfit to hold any responsible position, and for whom therefore posts are specially created, which though fictitious carry salaries of from six to ten thousand rubles that are not fictitious, and in receipt of which they live on to a great age.

Such was the Privy Councillor and superfluous member of various superfluous institutions, Ilya Epimovich Golovin.

He had three sons, of whom Ivan Ilych was the second. The eldest son was following in his father's footsteps only in another department, and was already approaching that stage in the service at which a similar sinecure would be reached. the third son was a failure. He had ruined his prospects in a number of positions and was not serving in the railway department. His father and brothers, and still more their wives, not merely disliked meeting him, but avoided remembering his existence unless compelled to do so. His sister had married Baron Greff, a Petersburg official of her father's type. Ivan Ilych was le phenix de la famille as people said. He was neither as cold and formal as his elder brother nor as wild as the younger, but was a happy mean between them – an intelligent polished, lively and agreeable man. He had studied with his younger brother at the School of

Law, but the latter had failed to complete the course and was expelled when he was in the fifth class. Ivan Ilych finished the course well. Even when he was at the School of Law he was just what he remained for the rest of his life: a capable, cheerful, good– natured, and sociable man, though strict in the fulfillment of what he considered to be his duty: and he considered his duty to be what was so considered by those in authority. Neither as a boy nor as a man was he a toady, but from early youth was by nature attracted to people of high station as a fly is drawn to the light, assimilating their ways and views of life and establishing friendly relations with them. All the enthusiasms of childhood and youth passed without leaving much trace on him; he succumbed to sensuality, to vanity, and latterly among the highest classes to liberalism, but always within limits which his instinct unfailingly indicated to him as correct.

At school he had done things which had formerly seemed to him very horrid and made him feel disgusted with himself when he did them; but when later on he saw that such actions were done by people of good position and that they did not regard them as wrong, he was able not exactly to regard them as right, but to forget about them entirely or not be at all troubled at remembering them.

Having graduated from the School of Law and qualified for the tenth rank of the civil service, and having received money from his father for his equipment, Ivan Ilych ordered himself clothes at Scharmer's, the fashionable tailor, hung a medallion inscribed respice finem on his watch–chain, took leave of his professor and the prince who was patron of the school, had a farewell dinner with his comrades at Donon's first– class restaurant, and with his new and fashionable portmanteau, linen, clothes, shaving and other toilet appliances, and a travelling rug, all purchased at the best shops, he set off for one of the provinces where through his father's influence, he had been attached to the governor as an official for special service.

In the province Ivan Ilych soon arranged as easy and agreeable a position for himself as he had had at the School of Law. He performed his official task, made his career, and at the same time amused himself pleasantly and decorously. Occasionally he paid official visits to country districts where he behaved with dignity both to his superiors and inferiors, and performed the duties entrusted to him, which related chiefly to the sectarians, with an exactness and incorruptible honesty of which he could not but feel proud.

In official matters, despite his youth and taste for frivolous gaiety, he was exceedingly reserved, punctilious, and even severe; but in society he was often amusing and witty, and always good– natured, correct in his manner, and bon enfant , as the governor and his wife – with whom he was like one of the family – used to say of him.

In the province he had an affair with a lady who made advances to the elegant young lawyer, and there was also a milliner; and there were carousals with aides– de– camp who visited the district, and after– supper visits to a certain outlying street of doubtful reputation; and there was too some obsequiousness to his chief and even to his chief's wife, but all this was done with such a tone of good breeding that no hard names could be applied to it. It all came under the heading of the French saying: "Il faut que jeunesse se passe." It was all done with clean hands, in clean linen, with French phrases, and above all among people of the best society and consequently with the approval of people of rank.

So Ivan Ilych served for five years and then came a change in his official life. The new and reformed judicial institutions were introduced, and new men were needed. Ivan Ilych became such a new man. He was offered the post of examining magistrate, and he accepted it though the post was in another province and obliged him to give up the connexions he had formed and to make new ones. His friends met to give him a send– off; they had a group photograph taken and presented him with a silver cigarette–case, and he set off to his new post.

As examining magistrate Ivan Ilych was just as comme il faut and decorous a man, inspiring general respect and capable of separating his official duties from his private life, as he had been when acting as an official on special service. His duties now as examining magistrate were fare more interesting and attractive than before. In his former position it had been pleasant to wear an undress uniform made by Scharmer, and to pass through the crowd of petitioners and officials who were timorously awaiting an audience with the governor, and who envied him as with free and easy gait he went straight into his chief's private room to have a cup of tea and a cigarette with him. But not many people had then been directly dependent on him – only police officials and the sectarians when he went on special missions – and he liked to treat them politely, almost as comrades, as if he were letting them feel that he who had the power to crush them was treating them in this simple, friendly way. There were then but few such people.

But now, as an examining magistrate, Ivan Ilych felt that everyone without exception, even the most important and self– satisfied, was in his power, and that he need only write a few words on a sheet of paper with a certain heading, and this or that important, self– satisfied person would be brought before him in the role of an accused person or a witness, and if he didnot choose to allow him to sit down, would have to stand before him and answer his questions. Ivan Ilych never abused his power; he tried on the contrary to soften its expression, but the consciousness of it and the possibility of softening its effect, supplied the chief interest and attraction of his office. In his work itself, especially in his examinations, he very soon acquired a method of eliminating all considerations irrelevant to the legal aspect of the case, and reducing even the most complicated case to a form in which it would be presented on paper only in its externals, completely excluding his personal opinion of the matter, while above all observing every prescribed formality. The work was new and Ivan Ilych was one of the first men to apply the new Code of 1864.

On taking up the post of examining magistrate in a new town, he made new acquaintances and connexions, placed himself on a new footing and assumed a somewhat different tone. He took up an attitude of rather dignified aloofness towards the provincial authorities, but picked out the best circle of legal gentlemen and wealthy gentry living in the town and assumed a tone of slight dissatisfaction with the government, of moderate liberalism, and of enlightened citizenship. At the same time, without at all altering the elegance of his toilet, he ceased shaving his chin and allowed his beard to grow as it pleased.

Ivan Ilych settled down very pleasantly in this new town. The society there, which inclined towards opposition to the governor was friendly, his salary was larger, and he began to play vint [a form of bridge], which he found added not a little to the pleasure of life, for he had a capacity for cards, played good– humouredly, and calculated rapidly and astutely, so that he usually won.

After living there for two years he met his future wife, Praskovya Fedorovna Mikhel, who was the most attractive, clever, and brilliant girl of the set in which he moved, and among other amusements and relaxations from his labours as examining magistrate, Ivan Ilych established light and playful relations with her.

While he had been an official on special service he had been accustomed to dance, but now as an examining magistrate it was exceptional for him to do so. If he danced now, he did it as if to show that though he served under the reformed order of things, and had reached the fifth official rank, yet when it came to dancing he could do it better than most people. So at the end of an evening he sometimes danced with Praskovya Fedorovna, and it was chiefly during these dances that he captivated her. She fell in love with him. Ivan Ilych had at first no definite intention of marrying, but when the girl fell in love with him he said to himself: "Really, why shouldn't I marry?"

Praskovya Fedorovna came of a good family, was not bad looking, and had some little property. Ivan Ilych might have aspired to a more brilliant match, but even this was good. He had his salary, and she, he hoped, would have an equal income. She was well connected, and was a sweet, pretty, and thoroughly correct young woman. to say that Ivan Ilych married because he fell in love with Praskovya Fedorovna and found that she sympathized with his views of life would be as incorrect as to say that he married because his social circle approved of the match. He was swayed by both these considerations: the marriage gave him personal satisfaction, and at the same time it was considered the right thing by the most highly placed of his associates.

So Ivan Ilych got married.

The preparations for marriage and the beginning of married life, with its conjugal caresses, the new furniture, new crockery, and new linen, were very pleasant until his wife became pregnant – so that Ivan Ilych had begun to think that marriage would not impair the easy, agreeable, gay and always decorous character of his life, approved of by society and regarded by himself as natural, but would even improve it. But from the first months of his wife's pregnancy, something new, unpleasant, depressing, and unseemly, and from which there was no way of escape, unexpectedly showed itself.

His wife, without any reason – de gaiete de coeur as Ivan Ilych expressed it to himself – began to disturb the pleasure and propriety of their life. She began to be jealous without any cause, expected him to devote his whole attention to her, found fault with everything, and made coarse and ill– mannered scenes.

At first Ivan Ilych hoped to escape from the unpleasantness of this state of affairs by the same easy and decorous relation to life that had served him heretofore: he tried to ignore his wife's disagreeable moods, continued to live in his usual easy and pleasant way, invited friends to his house for a game of cards, and also tried going out to his club or spending his evenings with friends. But one day his wife began upbraiding him so vigorously, using such coarse words, and continued to abuse him every time he did not fulfil her demands, so resolutely and with such evident determination not to give way till he submitted – that is, till he stayed at home and was bored just as she was – that he became alarmed. He now realized that matrimony – at any rate with Praskovya Fedorovna – was not always conducive to the pleasures and amenities of life, but on the contrary often infringed both comfort and propriety, and that he must therefore entrench himself against such infringement. And Ivan Ilych began to seek for means of doing so. His official duties were the one thing that imposed upon Praskovya Fedorovna, and by means of his official work and the duties attached to it he began struggling with his wife to secure his own independence.

With the birth of their child, the attempts to feed it and the various failures in doing so, and with the real and imaginary illnesses of mother and child, in which Ivan Ilych's sympathy was demanded but about which he understood nothing, the need of securing for himself an existence outside his family life became still more imperative.

As his wife grew more irritable and exacting and Ivan Ilych transferred the center of gravity of his life more and more to his official work, so did he grow to like his work better and became more ambitious than before.

Very soon, within a year of his wedding, Ivan Ilych had realized that marriage, though it may add some comforts to life, is in fact a very intricate and difficult affair towards which in order to perform one's duty, that is, to lead a decorous life approved of by society, one must adopt a definite attitude just as towards one's official duties.

And Ivan Ilych evolved such an attitude towards married life. He only required of it those conveniences – dinner at home, housewife, and bed – which it could give him, and above all that propriety of external forms required by public opinion. For the rest he looked for lighthearted pleasure and propriety, and was very thankful when he found them, but if he met with antagonism and querulousness he at once retired into his separate fenced– off world of official duties, where he found satisfaction.

Ivan Ilych was esteemed a good official, and after three years was made Assistant Public Prosecutor. His new duties, their importance, the possibility of indicting and imprisoning anyone he chose, the publicity his speeches received, and the success he had in all these things, made his work still more attractive.

More children came. His wife became more and more querulous and ill– tempered, but the attitude Ivan Ilych had adopted towards his home life rendered him almost impervious to her grumbling.

After seven years' service in that town he was transferred to another province as Public Prosecutor. They moved, but were short of money and his wife did not like the place they moved to. Though the salary was higher the cost of living was greater, besides which two of their children died and family life became still more unpleasant for him.

Praskovya Fedorovna blamed her husband for every inconvenience they encountered in their new home. Most of the conversations between husband and wife, especially as to the children's education, led to topics which recalled former disputes, and these disputes were apt to flare up again at any moment. There remained only those rare periods of amorousness which still came to them at times but did not last long. These were islets at which they anchored for a while and then again set out upon that ocean of veiled hostility which showed itself in their aloofness from one another. This aloofness might have grieved Ivan Ilych had he considered that it ought not to exist, but he now regarded the position as normal, and even made it the goal at which he aimed in family life. His aim was to free himself more and more from those unpleasantness and to give them a semblance of harmlessness and propriety. He attained this by spending less and less time with his family, and when obliged to be at home he tried to safeguard his position by the presence of outsiders. The chief thing however was that he had his official duties. The whole interest of his life now centered in the official world and that interest absorbed him. The consciousness of his power, being able to ruin anybody he wished to ruin, the importance, even the external dignity of his entry into court, or meetings with his subordinates, his success with superiors and inferiors, and above all his masterly handling of cases, of which he was conscious – all this gave him pleasure and filled his life, together with chats with his colleagues, dinners, and bridge. So that on the whole Ivan Ilych's life continued to flow as he considered it should do – pleasantly and properly.

So things continued for another seven years. His eldest daughter was already sixteen, another child had died, and only one son was left, a schoolboy and a subject of dissension. Ivan Ilych wanted to put him in the School of Law, but to spite him Praskovya Fedorovna entered him at the High School. The daughter had been educated at home and had turned out well: the boy did not learn badly either.

CHAPTER III

So Ivan Ilych lived for seventeen years after his marriage. He was already a Public Prosecutor of long standing, and had declined several proposed transfers while awaiting a more desirable post, when an unanticipated and unpleasant occurrence quite upset the peaceful course of his life. He was expecting to be offered the post of presiding judge in a University town, but Happe somehow came to the front and obtained the appointment instead. Ivan Ilych became irritable, reproached Happe, and quarrelled both him and with his immediate superiors – who became colder to him and again passed him over when other appointments were made.

This was in 1880, the hardest year of Ivan Ilych's life. It was then that it became evident on the one hand that his salary was insufficient for them to live on, and on the other that he had been forgotten, and not only this, but that what was for him the greatest and most cruel injustice appeared to others a quite ordinary occurrence. Even his father did not consider it his duty to help him. Ivan Ilych felt himself abandoned by everyone, and that they regarded his position with a salary of 3,500 rubles as quite normal and even fortunate. He alone knew that with the consciousness of the injustices done him, with his wife's incessant nagging, and with the debts he had contracted by living beyond his means, his position was far from normal.

In order to save money that summer he obtained leave of absence and went with his wife to live in the country at her brother's place.

In the country, without his work, he experienced ennui for the first time in his life, and not only ennui but intolerable depression, and he decided that it was impossible to go on living like that, and that it was necessary to take energetic measures.

Having passed a sleepless night pacing up and down the veranda, he decided to go to Petersburg and bestir himself, in order to punish those who had failed to appreciate him and to get transferred to another ministry.

Next day, despite many protests from his wife and her brother, he started for Petersburg with the sole object of obtaining a post with a salary of five thousand rubles a year. He was no longer bent on any particular department, or tendency, or kind of activity. All he now wanted was an appointment to another post with a salary of five thousand rubles, either in the administration, in the banks, with the railways in one of the Empress Marya's Institutions, or even in the customs – but it had to carry with it a salary of five thousand rubles and be in a ministry other than that in which they had failed to appreciate him.

And this quest of Ivan Ilych's was crowned with remarkable and unexpected success. At Kursk an acquaintance of his, F. I. Ilyin, got into the first– class carriage, sat down beside Ivan Ilych, and told him of a telegram just received by the governor of Kursk announcing that a change was about to take place in the ministry: Peter Ivanovich was to be superseded by Ivan Semonovich.

The proposed change, apart from its significance for Russia, had a special significance for Ivan Ilych, because by bringing forward a new man, Peter Petrovich, and consequently his friend Zachar Ivanovich, it was highly favourable for Ivan Ilych, since Sachar Ivanovich was a friend and colleague of his.

In Moscow this news was confirmed, and on reaching Petersburg Ivan Ilych found Zachar Ivanovich and received a definite promise of an appointment in his former Department of Justice.

A week later he telegraphed to his wife: "Zachar in Miller's place. I shall receive appointment on presentation of report."

Thanks to this change of personnel, Ivan Ilych had unexpectedly obtained an appointment in his former ministry which placed him two states above his former colleagues besides giving him five thousand rubles salary and three thousand five hundred rubles for expenses connected with his removal. All his ill humour towards his former enemies and the whole department vanished, and Ivan Ilych was completely happy.

He returned to the country more cheerful and contented than he had been for a long time. Praskovya Fedorovna also cheered up and a truce was arranged between them. Ivan Ilych told of how he had been feted by everybody in Petersburg, how all those who had been his enemies were put to shame and now fawned on him, how envious they were of his appointment, and how much everybody in Petersburg had liked him.

Praskovya Fedorovna listened to all this and appeared to believe it. She did not contradict anything, but only made plans for their life in the town to which they were going. Ivan Ilych saw with delight that these plans were his plans, that he and his wife agreed, and that, after a stumble, his life was regaining its due and natural character of pleasant lightheartedness and decorum.

Ivan Ilych had come back for a short time only, for he had to take up his new duties on the 10th of September. Moreover, he needed time to settle into the new place, to move all his belongings from the province, and to buy and order many additional things: in a word, to make such arrangements as he had resolved on, which were almost exactly what Praskovya Fedorovna too had decided on.

Now that everything had happened so fortunately, and that he and his wife were at one in their aims and moreover saw so little of one another, they got on together better than they had done since the first years of marriage. Ivan Ilych had thought of taking his family away with him at once, but the insistence of his wife's brother and her sister–in–law, who had suddenly become particularly amiable and friendly to him and his family, induced him to depart alone.

So he departed, and the cheerful state of mind induced by his success and by the harmony between his wife and himself, the one intensifying the other, did not leave him. He found a delightful house, just the thing both he and his wife had dreamt of. Spacious, lofty reception rooms in the old style, a convenient and dignified study, rooms for his wife and daughter, a study for his son – it might have been specially built for them. Ivan Ilych himself superintended the arrangements, chose the wallpapers, supplemented the furniture (preferably with antiques which he considered particularly comme il faut), and supervised the upholstering. Everything progressed and progressed and approached the ideal he had set himself: even when things were only half completed they exceeded his expectations. He saw what a refined and elegant character, free from vulgarity, it would all have when it was ready. On falling asleep he pictured to himself how the reception room would look. Looking at the yet unfinished drawing room he could see the fireplace, the screen, the what– not, the little chairs dotted here and there, the dishes and plates on the walls, and the bronzes, as they would be when everything was in place. He was pleased by the thought of how his wife and daughter, who shared his taste n this matter, would be impressed by it. They were certainly not expecting as much. He had been particularly successful in finding, and buying cheaply, antiques which gave a particularly aristocratic character to the whole place. But in his letters he intentionally understated everything in order to be able to surprise them. All this so absorbed him that his new duties – though he liked his official work – interested him less than he had expected. Sometimes he even had moments of absent– mindedness during the court sessions and would consider whether he should have straight or curved cornices for his curtains. He was so interested in it all that he often did things himself, rearranging the furniture, or rehanging the curtains. Once when mounting a step– ladder to show the upholsterer, who did not understand, how he wanted the hangings draped, he mad a false step and slipped, but being a strong and agile man he clung on and only knocked his side against the knob of the window frame. The bruised place was painful but the pain soon passed, and he felt particularly bright and well just then. He wrote: "I feel fifteen years younger." He thought he would have everything ready by September, but it dragged on till mid– October. But the result was charming not only in his eyes but to everyone who saw it.

In reality it was just what is usually seen in the houses of people of moderate means who want to appear rich, and therefore succeed only in resembling others like themselves: there are damasks, dark wood, plants, rugs, and dull and polished bronzes – all the things people of a certain class have in order to resemble other people of that class. His house was so like the others that it would never have been noticed, but to him it all seemed to be quite exceptional. He was very happy when he met his family at the station and brought them to the newly furnished house all lit up, where a footman in a white tie opened the door into the hall decorated with plants, and when they went on into the drawing– room and the study uttering exclamations of delight. He conducted them everywhere, drank in their praises eagerly, and beamed with pleasure. At tea that evening, when Praskovya Fedorovna among others things asked him about his fall, he laughed, and showed them how he had gone flying and had frightened the upholsterer.

"It's a good thing I'm a bit of an athlete. Another man might have been killed, but I merely knocked myself, just here; it hurts when it's touched, but it's passing off already – it's only a bruise."

So they began living in their new home – in which, as always happens, when they got thoroughly settled in they found they were just one room short – and with the increased income, which as always was just a little (some five hundred rubles) too little, but it was all very nice.

Things went particularly well at first, before everything was finally arranged and while something had still to be done: this thing bought, that thing ordered, another thing moved, and something else adjusted. Though there were some disputes between husband and wife, they were both so well satisfied and had so much to do that it all passed off without any serious quarrels. When nothing was left to arrange it became rather dull and something seemed to be lacking, but they were then making acquaintances, forming habits, and life was growing fuller.

Ivan Ilych spent his mornings at the law court and came home to diner, and at first he was generally in a good humour, though he occasionally became irritable just on account of his house. (Every spot on the tablecloth or the upholstery, and every broken window– blind string, irritated him. He had devoted so much trouble to arranging it all that every disturbance of it distressed him.) But on the whole his life ran its course as he believed life should do: easily, pleasantly, and decorously.

He got up at nine, drank his coffee, read the paper, and then put on his undress uniform and went to the law courts. there the harness in which he worked had already been stretched to fit him and he donned it without a hitch: petitioners, inquiries at the chancery, the chancery itself, and the sittings public and administrative. In all this the thing was to exclude everything fresh and vital, which always disturbs the regular course of official business, and to admit only official relations with people, and then only on official grounds. A man would come, for instance, wanting some information. Ivan Ilych, as one in whose sphere the matter did not lie, would have nothing to do with him: but if the man had some business with him in his official capacity, something that could be expressed on officially stamped paper, he would do everything, positively everything he could within the limits of such relations, and in doing so would maintain the semblance of friendly human relations, that is, would observe the courtesies of life. As soon as the official relations ended, so did everything else. Ivan Ilych possessed this capacity to separate his real life from the official side of affairs and not mix the two, in the highest degree, and by long practice and natural aptitude had brought it to such a pitch that sometimes, in the manner of a virtuoso, he would even allow himself to let the human and official relations mingle. He let himself do this just because he felt that he could at any time he chose resume the strictly official attitude again and drop the human relation. and he did it all easily, pleasantly, correctly, and even artistically. In the intervals between the sessions he smoked, drank tea, chatted a little about politics, a little about general topics, a little about cards, but most of all about official appointments. Tired, but with the feelings of a virtuoso – one of the first violins who has played his part in an orchestra with precision – he would return home to find that his wife and daughter had been out paying calls, or had a visitor, and that his son had been to school, had done his homework with his tutor, and was surely learning what is taught at High Schools. Everything was as it should be. After dinner, if they had no visitors, Ivan Ilych sometimes read a book that was being much discussed at the time, and in the evening settled down to work, that is, read official papers, compared the depositions of witnesses, and noted paragraphs of the Code applying to them. This was neither dull nor amusing. It was dull when he might have been playing bridge, but if no bridge was available it was at any rate better than doing nothing or sitting with his wife. Ivan Ilych's chief pleasure was giving little dinners to which he invited men and women of good social position, and just as his drawing– room resembled all other drawing– rooms so did his enjoyable little parties resemble all other such parties.

Once they even gave a dance. Ivan Ilych enjoyed it and everything went off well, except that it led to a violent quarrel with his wife about the cakes and sweets. Praskovya Fedorovna had made her own plans, but Ivan Ilych insisted on getting everything from an expensive confectioner and ordered too many cakes, and the quarrel occurred because some of those cakes were left over and the confectioner's bill came to forty– five rubles. It was a great and disagreeable quarrel. Praskovya Fedorovna called him "a fool and an imbecile," and he clutched at his head and made angry allusions to divorce.

But the dance itself had been enjoyable. The best people were there, and Ivan Ilych had danced with Princess Trufonova, a sister of the distinguished founder of the Society "Bear My Burden".

The pleasures connected with his work were pleasures of ambition; his social pleasures were those of vanity; but Ivan Ilych's greatest pleasure was playing bridge. He acknowledged that whatever disagreeable incident happened in his life, the pleasure that beamed like a ray of light above everything else was to sit down to bridge with good players, not noisy partners, and of course to four–handed bridge (with five players it was annoying to have to stand out, though one pretended not to mind), to play a clever and serious game (when the cards allowed it) and then to have supper and drink a glass of wine. after a game of bridge, especially if he had won a little (to win a large sum was unpleasant), Ivan Ilych went to bed in a specially good humour.

So they lived. They formed a circle of acquaintances among the best people and were visited by people of importance and by young folk. In their views as to their acquaintances, husband, wife and daughter were entirely agreed, and tacitly and unanimously kept at arm's length and shook off the various shabby friends and relations who, with much show of affection, gushed into the drawing– room with its Japanese plates on the walls. Soon these shabby friends ceased to obtrude themselves and only the best people remained in the Golovins' set.

Young men made up to Lisa, and Petrishchev, an examining magistrate and Dmitri Ivanovich Petrishchev's son and sole heir, began to be so attentive to her that Ivan Ilych had already spoken to Praskovya Fedorovna about it, and considered whether they should not arrange a party for them, or get up some private theatricals.

So they lived, and all went well, without change, and life flowed pleasantly.

CHAPTER IV

They were all in good health. It could not be called ill health if Ivan Ilych sometimes said that he had a queer taste in his mouth and felt some discomfort in his left side.

But this discomfort increased and, though not exactly painful, grew into a sense of pressure in his side accompanied by ill humour. And his irritability became worse and worse and began to mar the agreeable, easy, and correct life that had established itself in the Golovin family. Quarrels between husband and wife became more and more frequent, and soon the ease and amenity disappeared and even the decorum was barely maintained. Scenes again became frequent, and very few of those islets remained on which husband and wife could meet without an explosion. Praskovya Fedorovna now had good reason to say that her husband's temper was trying. With characteristic exaggeration she said he had always had a dreadful temper, and that it had needed all her good nature to put up with it for twenty years. It was true that now the quarrels were started by him. His bursts of temper always came just before dinner, often just as he began to eat his soup. Sometimes he noticed that a plate or dish was chipped, or the food was not right, or his son put his elbow on the table, or his daughter's hair was not done as he liked it, and for all this he blamed Praskovya Fedorovna. At first she retorted and said disagreeable things to him, but once or twice he fell into such a rage at the beginning of dinner that she realized it was due to some physical derangement brought on by taking food, and so she restrained herself and did not answer, but only hurried to get the dinner over. She regarded this self– restraint as highly praiseworthy. Having come to the conclusion that her husband had a dreadful temper and made her life miserable, she began to feel sorry for herself, and the more she pitied herself the more she hated her husband. She began to wish he would die; yet she did not want him to die because then his salary would cease. And this irritated her against him still more. She considered herself dreadfully unhappy just because not even his death could save her, and though she concealed her exasperation, that hidden exasperation of hers increased his irritation also.

After one scene in which Ivan Ilych had been particularly unfair and after which he had said in explanation that he certainly was irritable but that it was due to his not being well, she said that he was ill it should be attended to, and insisted on his going to see a celebrated doctor.

He went. Everything took place as he had expected and as it always does. There was the usual waiting and the important air assumed by the doctor, with which he was so familiar (resembling that which he himself assumed in court), and the sounding and listening, and the questions which called for answers that were foregone conclusions and were evidently unnecessary, and the look of importance which implied that "if only you put yourself in our hands we will arrange everything – we know indubitably how it has to be done, always in the same way for everybody alike." It was all just as it was in the law courts. The doctor put on just the same air towards him as he himself put on towards an accused person.

The doctor said that so– and– so indicated that there was so– and– so inside the patient, but if the investigation of so– and– so did not confirm this, then he must assume that and that. If he assumed that and that, then...and so on. To Ivan Ilych only one question was important: was his case serious or not? But the doctor ignored that inappropriate question. From his point of view it was not the one under consideration, the real question was to decide between a floating kidney, chronic catarrh, or appendicitis. It was not a question the doctor solved brilliantly, as it seemed to Ivan Ilych, in favour of the appendix, with the reservation that should an examination of the urine give fresh indications the matter would be reconsidered. All this was just what Ivan Ilych had himself brilliantly accomplished a thousand times in dealing with men on trial. The doctor summed up just as brilliantly, looking over his spectacles triumphantly and even gaily at the accused. From the doctor's summing up Ivan Ilych concluded that things were bad, but that for the doctor, and perhaps for everybody else, it was a matter of indifference, though for him it was bad. And this conclusion struck him painfully, arousing in him a great feeling of pity for himself and of bitterness towards the doctor's indifference to a matter of such importance.

He said nothing of this, but rose, placed the doctor's fee on the table, and remarked with a sigh: "We sick people probably often put inappropriate questions. But tell me, in general, is this complaint dangerous, or not?..."

The doctor looked at him sternly over his spectacles with one eye, as if to say: "Prisoner, if you will not keep to the questions put to you, I shall be obliged to have you removed from the court."

"I have already told you what I consider necessary and proper. The analysis may show something more." And the doctor bowed.

Ivan Ilych went out slowly, seated himself disconsolately in his sledge, and drove home. All the way home he was going over what the doctor had said, trying to translate those complicated, obscure, scientific phrases into plain language and find in them an answer to the question: "Is my condition bad? Is it very bad? Or is there as yet nothing much wrong?" And it seemed to him that the meaning of what the doctor had said was that it was very bad. Everything in the streets seemed depressing. The cabmen, the houses, the passers– by, and the shops, were dismal. His ache, this dull gnawing ache that never ceased for a moment, seemed to have acquired a new and more serious significance from the doctor's dubious remarks. Ivan Ilych now watched it with a new and oppressive feeling.

He reached home and began to tell his wife about it. She listened, but in the middle of his account his daughter came in with her hat on, ready to go out with her mother. She sat down reluctantly to listen to this tedious story, but could not stand it long, and her mother too did not hear him to the end.

"Well, I am very glad," she said. "Mind now to take your medicine regularly. Give me the prescription and I'll send Gerasim to the chemist's." And she went to get ready to go out.

While she was in the room Ivan Ilych had hardly taken time to breathe, but he sighed deeply when she left it.

"Well," he thought, "perhaps it isn't so bad after all."

He began taking his medicine and following the doctor's directions, which had been altered after the examination of the urine. but then it happened that there was a contradiction between the indications drawn from the examination of the urine and the symptoms that showed themselves. It turned out that what was happening differed from what the doctor had told him, and that he had either forgotten or blundered, or hidden something from him. He could not, however, be blamed for that, and Ivan Ilych still obeyed his orders implicitly and at first derived some comfort from doing so.

From the time of his visit to the doctor, Ivan Ilych's chief occupation was the exact fulfillment of the doctor's instructions regarding hygiene and the taking of medicine, and the observation of his pain and his excretions. His chief interest came to be people's ailments and people's health. When sickness, deaths, or recoveries were mentioned in his presence, especially when the illness resembled his own, he listened with agitation which he tried to hide, asked questions, and applied what he heard to his own case.

The pain did not grow less, but Ivan Ilych made efforts to force himself to think that he was better. And he could do this so long as nothing agitated him. But as soon as he had any unpleasantness with his wife, any lack of success in his official work, or held bad cards at bridge, he was at once acutely sensible of his disease. He had formerly borne such mischances, hoping soon to adjust what was wrong, to master it and attain success, or make a grand slam. But now every mischance upset him and plunged him into despair. He would say to himself: "there now, just as I was beginning to get better and the medicine had begun to take effect, comes this accursed misfortune, or unpleasantness..." And he was furious with the mishap, or with the people who were causing the unpleasantness and killing him, for he felt that this fury was killing him but he could not restrain it. One would have thought that it should have been clear to him that this exasperation with circumstances and people aggravated his illness, and that he ought therefore to ignore unpleasant occurrences. But he drew the very opposite conclusion: he said that he needed peace, and he watched for everything that might disturb it and became irritable at the slightest infringement of it. His condition was rendered worse by the fact that he read medical books and consulted doctors. The progress of his disease was so gradual that he could deceive himself when comparing one day with another – the difference was so slight. But when he consulted the doctors it seemed to him that he was getting worse, and even very rapidly. Yet despite this he was continually consulting them.

That month he went to see another celebrity, who told him almost the same as the first had done but put his questions rather differently, and the interview with this celebrity only increased Ivan Ilych's doubts and fears. A friend of a friend of his, a very good doctor, diagnosed his illness again quite differently from the others, and though he predicted recovery, his questions and suppositions bewildered Ivan Ilych still more and increased his doubts. A homeopathist diagnosed the disease in yet another way, and prescribed medicine which Ivan Ilych took secretly for a week. But after a week, not feeling any improvement and having lost confidence both in the former doctor's treatment and in this one's, he became still more despondent. One day a lady acquaintance mentioned a cure effected by a wonder-working icon. Ivan Ilych caught himself listening attentively and beginning to believe that it had occurred. This incident alarmed him. "Has my mind really weakened to such an extent?" he asked himself. "Nonsense! It's all rubbish. I mustn't give way to nervous fears but having chosen a doctor must keep strictly to his treatment. That is what I will do. Now it's all settled. I won't think about it, but will follow the treatment seriously till summer, and then we shall see. From now there must be no more of this wavering!" this was easy to say but impossible to carry out. The pain in his side oppressed him and seemed to grow worse and more incessant, while the taste in his mouth grew stranger and stranger. It seemed to him that his breath had a disgusting smell, and he was conscious of a loss of appetite and strength. There was no deceiving himself: something terrible, new, and more important than anything before in his life, was taking place within him of which he alone was aware. Those about him did not understand or would not understand it, but thought everything in the world was going on as usual. That tormented Ivan Ilych more than anything. He saw that his household, especially his wife and daughter who were in a perfect whirl of visiting, did not understand anything of it and were annoyed that he was so depressed and so exacting, as if he were to blame for it. Though they tried to disguise it he saw that he was an obstacle in their path, and that his wife had adopted a definite line in regard to his illness and kept to it regardless of anything he said or did. Her attitude was this: "You know," she would say to her friends, "Ivan Ilych can't do as other people do, and keep to the treatment prescribed for him. One day he'll take his drops and keep strictly to his diet and go to bed in good time, but the next day unless I watch him he'll suddenly forget his medicine, eat sturgeon – which is forbidden – and sit up playing cards till one o'clock in the morning."

"Oh, come, when was that?" Ivan Ilych would ask in vexation. "Only once at Peter Ivanovich's."

"And yesterday with shebek."

"Well, even if I hadn't stayed up, this pain would have kept me awake."

"Be that as it may you'll never get well like that, but will always make us wretched."

Praskovya Fedorovna's attitude to Ivan Ilych's illness, as she expressed it both to others and to him, was that it was his own fault and was another of the annoyances he caused her. Ivan ilych felt that this opinion escaped her involuntarily – but that did not make it easier for him.

At the law courts too, Ivan Ilych noticed, or thought he noticed, a strange attitude towards himself. It sometimes seemed to him that people were watching him inquisitively as a man whose place might soon be vacant. Then again, his friends would suddenly begin to chaff him in a friendly way about his low spirits, as if the awful, horrible, and unheard-of thing that was going on within him, incessantly gnawing at him and irresistibly drawing him away, was a very agreeable subject for jests. Schwartz in particular irritated him by his jocularity, vivacity, and savoir– faire , which reminded him of what he himself had been ten years ago.

Friends came to make up a set and they sat down to cards. They dealt, bending the new cards to soften them, and he sorted the diamonds in his hand and found he had seven. His partner said "No trumps" and supported him with two diamonds. What more could be wished for? It ought to be jolly and lively. They would make a grand slam. But suddenly Ivan Ilych was conscious of that gnawing pain, that taste in his mouth, and it seemed ridiculous that in such circumstances he should be pleased to make a grand slam.

He looked at his partner Mikhail Mikhaylovich, who rapped the table with his strong hand and instead of snatching up the tricks pushed the cards courteously and indulgently towards Ivan Ilych that he might have the pleasure of gathering them up without the trouble of stretching out his hand for them. "Does he think I am too weak to stretch out my arm?" thought Ivan Ilych, and forgetting what he was doing he over– trumped his partner, missing the grand slam by three tricks. And what was most awful of all was that he saw how upset Mikhail Mikhaylovich was about it but did not himself care. And it was dreadful to realize why he did not care.

They all saw that he was suffering, and said: "We can stop if you are tired. Take a rest." Lie down? No, he was not at all tired, and he finished the rubber. All were gloomy and silent. Ivan Ilych felt that he had diffused this gloom over them and could not dispel it. They had supper and went away, and Ivan Ilych was left alone with the consciousness that his life was poisoned and was poisoning the lives of others, and that this poison did not weaken but penetrated more and more deeply into his whole being.

With this consciousness, and with physical pain besides the terror, he must go to bed, often to lie awake the greater part of the night. Next morning he had to get up again, dress, go to the law courts, speak, and write; or if he did not go out, spend at home those twenty– four hours a day each of which was a torture. And he had to live thus all alone on the brink of an abyss, with no one who understood or pitied him.

CHAPTER V

So one month passed and then another. Just before the New Year his brother– in– law came to town and stayed at their house. Ivan Ilych was at the law courts and Praskovya Fedorovna had gone shopping. When Ivan Ilych came home and entered his study he found his brother– in– law there – a healthy, florid man – unpacking his portmanteau himself. He raised his head on hearing Ivan Ilych's footsteps and looked up at him for a moment without a word. That stare told Ivan Ilych everything. His brother– in– law opened his mouth to utter an exclamation of surprise but checked himself, and that action confirmed it all. "I have changed, eh?" "Yes, there is a change." And after that, try as he would to get his brother– in– law to return to the subject of his looks, the latter would say nothing about it. Praskovya Fedorovna came home and her brother went out to her. Ivan Ilych locked to door and began to examine himself in the glass, first full face, then in profile. He took up a portrait of himself taken with his wife, and compared it with what he saw in the glass. The change in him was immense. Then he bared his arms to the elbow, looked at them, drew the sleeves down again, sat down on an ottoman, and grew blacker than night.

"No, no, this won't do!" he said to himself, and jumped up, went to the table, took up some law papers and began to read them, but could not continue. He unlocked the door and went into the reception– room. The door leading to the drawing– room was shut. He approached it on tiptoe and listened.

"No, you are exaggerating!" Praskovya Fedorovna was saying.

"Exaggerating! Don't you see it? Why, he's a dead man! Look at his eyes – there's no life in them. But what is it that is wrong with him?"

"No one knows. Nikolaevich [that was another doctor] said something, but I don't know what. And Seshchetitsky [this was the celebrated specialist] said quite the contrary..."

Ivan Ilych walked away, went to his own room, lay down, and began musing; "The kidney, a floating kidney." He recalled all the doctors had told him of how it detached itself and swayed about. And by an effort of imagination he tried to catch that kidney and arrest it and support it. So little was needed for this, it seemed to him. "No, I'll go to see Peter Ivanovich again." [That was the friend whose friend was a doctor.] He rang, ordered the carriage, and got ready to go.

"Where are you going, Jean?" asked his wife with a specially sad and exceptionally kind look.

This exceptionally kind look irritated him. He looked morosely at her.

"I must go to see Peter Ivanovich."

He went to see Peter Ivanovich, and together they went to see his friend, the doctor. He was in, and Ivan Ilych had a long talk with him.

Reviewing the anatomical and physiological details of what in the doctor's opinion was going on inside him, he understood it all.

There was something, a small thing, in the vermiform appendix. It might all come right. Only stimulate the energy of one organ and check the activity of another, then absorption would take place and everything would come right. He got home rather late for dinner, ate his dinner, and conversed cheerfully, but could not for a long time bring himself to go back to work in his room. At last, however, he went to his study and did what was necessary, but the consciousness that he had put something aside – an important, intimate matter which he would revert to when his work was done – never left him. When he had finished his work he remembered that this intimate matter was the thought of his vermiform appendix. But he did not give himself up to it, and went to the drawing– room for tea. There were callers there, including the examining magistrate who was a desirable match for his daughter, and they were conversing, playing the piano, and singing. Ivan Ilych, as Praskovya Fedorovna remarked, spent that evening more cheerfully than usual, but he never for a moment forgot that he had postponed the important matter of the appendix. At eleven o'clock he said goodnight and went to his bedroom. Since his illness he had slept alone in a small room next to his study. He undressed and took up a novel by Zola, but instead of reading it he fell into thought, and in his imagination that desired improvement in the vermiform appendix occurred. There was the absorption and evacuation and the re– establishment of normal activity. "Yes, that's it!" he said to himself. "One need only assist nature, that's all." He remembered his medicine, rose, took it, and lay down on his back watching for the beneficent action of the medicine and for it to lessen the pain. "I need only take it regularly and avoid all injurious influences. I am already feeling better, much better." He began touching his side: it was not painful to the touch. "There, I really don't feel it. It's much better already." He put out the light and turned on his side ... "The appendix is getting better, absorption is occurring." Suddenly he felt the old, familiar, dull, gnawing pain, stubborn and serious. There was the same familiar loathsome taste in his mouth. His heart sand and he felt dazed. "My God! My God!" he muttered. "Again, again! And it will never cease." And suddenly the matter presented itself in a quite different aspect. "Vermiform appendix! Kidney!" he said to himself. "It's not a question of appendix or kidney, but of life and...death. Yes, life was there and now it is going, going and I cannot stop it. Yes. Why deceive myself? Isn't it obvious to everyone but me that I'm dying, and that it's only a question of weeks, days...it may happen this moment. There was light and now there is darkness. I was here and now I'm going there! Where?" A chill came over him, his breathing ceased, and he felt only the throbbing of his heart.

"When I am not, what will there be? There will be nothing. Then where shall I be when I am no more? Can this be dying? No, I don't want to!" He jumped up and tried to light the candle, felt for it with trembling hands, dropped candle and candlestick on the floor, and fell back on his pillow.

"What's the use? It makes no difference," he said to himself, staring with wide– open eyes into the darkness. "Death. Yes, death. And none of them knows or wishes to know it, and they have no pity for me. Now they are playing." (He heard through the door the distant sound of a song and its accompaniment.) "It's all the same to them, but they will die too! Fools! I first, and they later, but it will be the same for them. And now they are merry...the beasts!"

Anger choked him and he was agonizingly, unbearably miserable. "It is impossible that all men have been doomed to suffer this awful horror!" He raised himself.

"Something must be wrong. I must calm myself – must think it all over from the beginning." And he again began thinking. "Yes, the beginning of my illness: I knocked my side, but I was still quite well that day and the next. It hurt a little, then rather more. I saw the doctors, then followed despondency and anguish, more doctors, and I drew nearer to the abyss. My strength grew less and I kept coming nearer and nearer, and now I have wasted away and there is no light in my eyes. I think of the appendix – but this is death! I think of mending the appendix, and all the while here is death! Can it really be death?" Again terror seized him and he gasped for breath. He leant down and began feeling for the matches, pressing with his elbow on the stand beside the bed. It was in his way and hurt him, he grew furious with it, pressed on it still harder, and upset it. Breathless and in despair he fell on his back, expecting death to come immediately.

Meanwhile the visitors were leaving. Praskovya Fedorovna was seeing them off. She heard something fall and came in.

"What has happened?"

"Nothing. I knocked it over accidentally."

She went out and returned with a candle. He lay there panting heavily, like a man who has run a thousand yards, and stared upwards at her with a fixed look.

"What is it, Jean?"

"No...o...thing. I upset it." ("Why speak of it? She won't understand," he thought.)

And in truth she did not understand. She picked up the stand, lit his candle, and hurried away to see another visitor off. When she came back he still lay on his back, looking upwards.

"What is it? Do you feel worse?"

"Yes."

She shook her head and sat down.

"Do you know, Jean, I think we must ask Leshchetitsky to come and see you here."

This meant calling in the famous specialist, regardless of expense. He smiled malignantly and said "No." She remained a little longer and then went up to him and kissed his forehead.

While she was kissing him he hated her from the bottom of his soul and with difficulty refrained from pushing her away.

"Good night. Please God you'll sleep."

"Yes."

CHAPTER VI

Ivan Ilych saw that he was dying, and he was in continual despair.

In the depth of his heart he knew he was dying, but not only was he not accustomed to the thought, he simply did not and could not grasp it.

The syllogism he had learnt from Kiesewetter's Logic: "Caius is a man, men are mortal, therefore Caius is mortal," had always seemed to him correct as applied to Caius, but certainly not as applied to himself. That Caius – man in the abstract – was mortal, was perfectly correct, but he was not Caius, not an abstract man, but a creature quite, quite separate from all others. He had been little Vanya, with a mamma and a papa, with Mitya and Volodya, with the toys, a coachman and a nurse, afterwards with Katenka and will all the joys, griefs, and delights of childhood, boyhood, and youth. What did Caius know of the smell of that striped leather ball Vanya had been so fond of? Had Caius kissed his mother's hand like that, and did the silk of her dress rustle so for Caius? Had he rioted like that at school when the pastry was bad? Had Caius been in love like that?

Could Caius preside at a session as he did? "Caius really was mortal, and it was right for him to die; but for me, little Vanya, Ivan Ilych, with all my thoughts and emotions, it's altogether a different matter. It cannot be that I ought to die. That would be too terrible."

Such was his feeling.

"If I had to die like Caius I would have known it was so. An inner voice would have told me so, but there was nothing of the sort in me and I and all my friends felt that our case was quite different from that of Caius. and now here it is!" he said to himself. "It can't be. It's impossible! But here it is. How is this? How is one to understand it?"

He could not understand it, and tried to drive this false, incorrect, morbid thought away and to replace it by other proper and healthy thoughts. But that thought, and not the thought only but the reality itself, seemed to come and confront him.

And to replace that thought he called up a succession of others, hoping to find in them some support. He tried to get back into the former current of thoughts that had once screened the thought of death from him. But strange to say, all that had formerly shut off, hidden, and destroyed his consciousness of death, no longer had that effect. Ivan Ilych now spent most of his time in attempting to re– establish that old current. He would say to himself: "I will take up my duties again – after all I used to live by them." And banishing all doubts he would go to the law courts, enter into conversation with his colleagues, and sit carelessly as was his wont, scanning the crowd with a thoughtful look and leaning both his emaciated arms on the arms of his oak chair; bending over as usual to a colleague and drawing his papers nearer he would interchange whispers with him, and then suddenly raising his eyes and sitting erect would pronounce certain words and open the proceedings. But suddenly in the midst of those proceedings the pain in his side, regardless of the stage the proceedings had reached, would begin its own gnawing work. Ivan Ilych would turn his attention to it and try to drive the thought of it away, but without success. It would come and stand before him and look at him, and he would be petrified and the light would die out of his eyes, and he would again begin asking himself whether It alone was true. And his colleagues and subordinates would see with surprise and distress that he, the brilliant and subtle judge, was becoming confused and making mistakes. He would shake himself, try to pull himself together, manage somehow to bring the sitting to a close, and return home with the sorrowful consciousness that his judicial labours could not as formerly hide from him what he wanted them to hide, and could not deliver him from It . And what was worst of all was that It drew his attention to itself not in order to make him take some action but only that he should look at It , look it straight in the face: look at it and without doing anything, suffer inexpressibly.

And to save himself from this condition Ivan Ilych looked for consolations – new screens – and new screens were found and for a while seemed to save him, but then they immediately fell to pieces or rather became transparent, as if It penetrated them and nothing could veil It .

In these latter days he would go into the drawing–room he had arranged – that drawing– room where he had fallen and for the sake of which (how bitterly ridiculous it seemed) he had sacrificed his life – for he knew that his illness originated with that knock. He would enter and see that something had scratched the polished table. He would look for the cause of this and find that it was the bronze ornamentation of an album, that had got bent. He would take up the expensive album which he had lovingly arranged, and feel vexed with his daughter and her friends for their untidiness – for the album was torn here and there and some of the photographs turned upside down. He would put it carefully in order and bend the ornamentation back into position. Then it would occur to him to place all those things in another corner of the room, near the plants. He would call the footman, but his daughter or wife would come to help him. They would not agree, and his wife would contradict him, and he would dispute and grow angry. But that was all right, for then he did not think about It . It was invisible.

But then, when he was moving something himself, his wife would say: "Let the servants do it. You will hurt yourself again." And suddenly It would flash through the screen and he would see it. It was just a flash, and he hoped it would disappear, but he would involuntarily pay attention to his side. "It sits there as before, gnawing just the same!" And he could no longer forget It , but could distinctly see it looking at him from behind the flowers. "What is it all for?"

"It really is so! I lost my life over that curtain as I might have done when storming a fort. Is that possible? How terrible and how stupid. It can't be true! It can't, but it is."

He would go to his study, lie down, and again be alone with It : face to face with It . And nothing could be done with It except to look at it and shudder.

CHAPTER VII

How it happened it is impossible to say because it came about step by step, unnoticed, but in the third month of Ivan Ilych's illness, his wife, his daughter, his son, his acquaintances, the doctors, the servants, and above all he himself, were aware that the whole interest he had for other people was whether he would soon vacate his place, and at last release the living from the discomfort caused by his presence and be himself released from his sufferings.

He slept less and less. He was given opium and hypodermic injections of morphine, but this did not relieve him. The dull depression he experienced in a somnolent condition at first gave him a little relief, but only as something new, afterwards it became as distressing as the pain itself or even more so.

Special foods were prepared for him by the doctors' orders, but all those foods became increasingly distasteful and disgusting to him.

For his excretions also special arrangements had to be made, and this was a torment to him every time – a torment from the uncleanliness, the unseemliness, and the smell, and from knowing that another person had to take part in it.

But just through his most unpleasant matter, Ivan Ilych obtained comfort. Gerasim, the butler's young assistant, always came in to carry the things out. Gerasim was a clean, fresh peasant lad, grown stout on town food and always cheerful and bright. At first the sight of him, in his clean Russian peasant costume, engaged on that disgusting task embarrassed Ivan Ilych.

Once when he got up from the commode to weak to draw up his trousers, he dropped into a soft armchair and looked with horror at his bare, enfeebled thighs with the muscles so sharply marked on them.

Gerasim with a firm light tread, his heavy boots emitting a pleasant smell of tar and fresh winter air, came in wearing a clean Hessian apron, the sleeves of his print shirt tucked up over his strong bare young arms; and refraining from looking at his sick master out of consideration for his feelings, and restraining the joy of life that beamed from his face, he went up to the commode.

"Gerasim!" said Ivan Ilych in a weak voice.

"Gerasim started, evidently afraid he might have committed some blunder, and with a rapid movement turned his fresh, kind, simple young face which just showed the first downy signs of a beard.

"Yes, sir?"

"That must be very unpleasant for you. You must forgive me. I am helpless."

"Oh, why, sir," and Gerasim's eyes beamed and he showed his glistening white teeth, "what's a little trouble? It's a case of illness with you, sir."

And his deft strong hands did their accustomed task, and he went out of the room stepping lightly. five minutes later he as lightly returned.

Ivan Ilych was still sitting in the same position in the armchair.

"Gerasim," he said when the latter had replaced the freshly– washed utensil. "Please come here and help me." Gerasim went up to him. "Lift me up. It is hard for me to get up, and I have sent Dmitri away."

Gerasim went up to him, grasped his master with his strong arms deftly but gently, in the same way that he stepped – lifted him, supported him with one hand, and with the other drew up his trousers and would have set him down again, but Ivan Ilych asked to be led to the sofa. Gerasim, without an effort and without apparent pressure, led him, almost lifting him, to the sofa and placed him on it.

"That you. How easily and well you do it all!"

Gerasim smiled again and turned to leave the room. But Ivan Ilych felt his presence such a comfort that he did not want to let him go.

"One thing more, please move up that chair. No, the other one – under my feet. It is easier for me when my feet are raised."

Gerasim brought the chair, set it down gently in place, and raised Ivan Ilych's legs on it. It seemed to Ivan Ilych that he felt better while Gerasim was holding up his legs.

"It's better when my legs are higher," he said. "Place that cushion under them."

Gerasim did so. He again lifted the legs and placed them, and again Ivan Ilych felt better while Gerasim held his legs. When he set them down Ivan Ilych fancied he felt worse.

"Gerasim," he said. "Are you busy now?"

"Not at all, sir," said Gerasim, who had learnt from the townsfolk how to speak to gentlefolk.

"What have you still to do?"

"What have I to do? I've done everything except chopping the logs for tomorrow."

"Then hold my legs up a bit higher, can you?"

"Of course I can. Why not?" and Gerasim raised his master's legs higher and Ivan Ilych thought that in that position he did not feel any pain at all.

"And how about the logs?"

"Don't trouble about that, sir. There's plenty of time."

Ivan Ilych told Gerasim to sit down and hold his legs, and began to talk to him. And strange to say it seemed to him that he felt better while Gerasim held his legs up.

After that Ivan Ilych would sometimes call Gerasim and get him to hold his legs on his shoulders, and he liked talking to him. Gerasim did it all easily, willingly, simply, and with a good nature that touched Ivan Ilych. Health, strength, and vitality in other people were offensive to him, but Gerasim's strength and vitality did not mortify but soothed him.

What tormented Ivan Ilych most was the deception, the lie, which for some reason they all accepted, that he was not dying but was simply ill, and the only need keep quiet and undergo a treatment and then something very good would result. He however knew that do what they would nothing would come of it, only still more agonizing suffering and death. This deception tortured him – their not wishing to admit what they all knew and what he knew, but wanting to lie to him concerning his terrible condition, and wishing and forcing him to participate in that lie. Those lies – lies enacted over him on the eve of his death and destined to degrade this awful, solemn act to the level of their visitings, their curtains, their sturgeon for dinner – were a terrible agony for Ivan Ilych. And strangely enough, many times when they were going through their antics over him he had been within a hairbreadth of calling out to them: "Stop lying! You know and I know that I am dying. Then at least stop lying about it!" But he had never had the spirit to do it. The awful, terrible act of his dying was, he could see, reduced by those about him to the level of a casual, unpleasant, and almost indecorous incident (as if someone entered a drawing room defusing an unpleasant odour) and this was done by that very decorum which he had served all his life long. He saw that no one felt for him, because no one even wished to grasp his position. Only Gerasim recognized it and pitied him. And so Ivan Ilych felt at ease only with him. He felt comforted when Gerasim supported his legs (sometimes all night long) and refused to go to bed, saying: "Don't you worry, Ivan Ilych. I'll get sleep enough later on," or when he suddenly became familiar and exclaimed: "If you weren't sick it would be another matter, but as it is, why should I grudge a little trouble?" Gerasim alone did not lie; everything showed that he alone understood the facts of the case and did not consider it necessary to disguise them, but simply felt sorry for his emaciated and enfeebled master. Once when Ivan Ilych was sending him away he even said straight out: "We shall all of us die, so why should I grudge a little trouble?" – expressing the fact that he did not think his work burdensome, because he was doing it for a dying man and hoped someone would do the same for him when his time came.

Apart from this lying, or because of it, what most tormented Ivan Ilych was that no one pitied him as he wished to be pitied. At certain moments after prolonged suffering he wished most of all (though he would have been ashamed to confess it) for someone to pity him as a sick child is pitied. He longed to be petted and comforted. he knew he was an important functionary, that he had a beard turning grey, and that therefore what he long for was impossible, but still he longed for it. and in Gerasim's attitude towards him there was something akin to what he wished for, and so that attitude comforted him. Ivan Ilych wanted to weep, wanted to be petted and cried over, and then his colleague Shebek would come, and instead of weeping and being petted, Ivan

Ilych would assume a serious, severe, and profound air, and by force of habit would express his opinion on a decision of the Court of Cassation and would stubbornly insist on that view. This falsity around him and within him did more than anything else to poison his last days.

Chapter VIII

It was morning. He knew it was morning because Gerasim had gone, and Peter the footman had come and put out the candles, drawn back one of the curtains, and begun quietly to tidy up. Whether it was morning or evening, Friday or Sunday, made no difference, it was all just the same: the gnawing, unmitigated, agonizing pain, never ceasing for an instant, the consciousness of life inexorably waning but not yet extinguished, the approach of that ever dreaded and hateful Death which was the only reality, and always the same falsity. What were days, weeks, hours, in such a case?

"Will you have some tea, sir?"

"He wants things to be regular, and wishes the gentlefolk to drink tea in the morning," thought ivan Ilych, and only said "No."

"Wouldn't you like to move onto the sofa, sir?"

"He wants to tidy up the room, and I'm in the way. I am uncleanliness and disorder," he thought, and said only:

"No, leave me alone."

The man went on bustling about. Ivan Ilych stretched out his hand. Peter came up, ready to help.

"What is it, sir?"

"My watch."

Peter took the watch which was close at hand and gave it to his master.

"Half– past eight. Are they up?"

"No sir, except Vladimir Ivanovich" (the son) "who has gone to school. Praskovya Fedorovna ordered me to wake her if you asked for her. Shall I do so?"

"No, there's no need to." "Perhaps I's better have some tea," he thought, and added aloud: "Yes, bring me some tea."

Peter went to the door, but Ivan Ilych dreaded being left alone. "How can I keep him here? Oh yes, my medicine." "Peter, give me my medicine." "Why not? Perhaps it may still do some good." He took a spoonful and swallowed it. "No, it won't help. It's all tomfoolery, all deception," he decided as soon as he became aware of the familiar, sickly, hopeless taste. "No, I can't believe in it any longer. But the pain, why this pain? If it would only cease just for a moment!" And he moaned. Peter turned towards him. "It's all right. Go and fetch me some tea."

Peter went out. Left alone Ivan Ilych groaned not so much with pain, terrible thought that was, as from mental anguish. Always and for ever the same, always these endless days and nights. If only it would come quicker! If only what would come quicker? Death, darkness?...No, no! anything rather than death!

when Peter returned with the tea on a tray, Ivan Ilych stared at him for a time in perplexity, not realizing who and what he was. Peter was disconcerted by that look and his embarrassment brought Ivan Ilych to himself.

"Oh, tea! All right, put it down. Only help me to wash and put on a clean shirt."

And Ivan Ilych began to wash. With pauses for rest, he washed his hands and then his face, cleaned his teeth, brushed his hair, looked in the glass. He was terrified by what he saw, especially by the limp way in which his hair clung to his pallid forehead.

While his shirt was being changed he knew that he would be still more frightened at the sight of his body, so he avoided looking at it. Finally he was ready. He drew on a dressing– gown, wrapped himself in a plaid, and sat down in the armchair to take his tea. For a moment he felt refreshed, but as soon as he began to drink the tea he was again aware of the same taste, and the pain also returned. He finished it with an effort, and then lay down stretching out his legs, and dismissed Peter.

Always the same. Now a spark of hope flashes up, then a sea of despair rages, and always pain; always pain, always despair, and always the same. When alone he had a dreadful and distressing desire to call someone, but he knew beforehand that with others present it would be still worse. "Another dose of morphine–to lose consciousness. I will tell him, the doctor, that he must think of something else. It's impossible, impossible, to go on like this."

An hour and another pass like that. But now there is a ring at the door bell. Perhaps it's the doctor? It is. He comes in fresh, hearty, plump, and cheerful, with that look on his face that seems to say: "There now, you're in a panic about something, but we'll arrange it all for you directly!" The doctor knows this expression is out of place here, but he has put it on once for all and can't take it off– like a man who has put on a frock– coat in the morning to pay a round of calls.

The doctor rubs his hands vigorously and reassuringly.

"Brr! How cold it is! There's such a sharp frost; just let me warm myself!" he says, as if it were only a matter of waiting till he was warm, and then he would put everything right.

"Well now, how are you?"

Ivan Ilych feels that the doctor would like to say: "Well, how are our affairs?" but that even he feels that this would not do, and says instead: "What sort of a night have you had?"

Ivan Ilych looks at him as much as to say: "Are you really never ashamed of lying?" But the doctor does not wish to understand this question, and Ivan Ilych says: "Just as terrible as ever. The pain never leaves me and never subsides. If only something ... "

"Yes, you sick people are always like that.... There, now I think I am warm enough. Even Praskovya Fedorovna, who is so particular, could find no fault with my temperature. Well, now I can say good– morning," and the doctor presses his patient's hand.

Then dropping his former playfulness, he begins with a most serious face to examine the patient, feeling his pulse and taking his temperature, and then begins the sounding and auscultation.

Ivan Ilych knows quite well and definitely that all this is nonsense and pure deception, but when the doctor, getting down on his knee, leans over him, putting his ear first higher then lower, and performs various gymnastic movements over him with a significant expression on his face, Ivan Ilych submits to it all as he used to submit to the speeches of the lawyers, though he knew very well that they were all lying and why they were lying.

The doctor, kneeling on the sofa, is still sounding him when Praskovya Fedorovna's silk dress rustles at the door and she is heard scolding Peter for not having let her know of the doctor's arrival.

She comes in, kisses her husband, and at once proceeds to prove that she has been up a long time already, and only owing to a misunderstanding failed to be there when the doctor arrived.

Ivan Ilych looks at her, scans her all over, sets against her the whiteness and plumpness and cleanness of her hands and neck, the gloss of her hair, and the sparkle of her vivacious eyes. He hates her with his whole soul. And the thrill of hatred he feels for her makes him suffer from her touch.

Her attitude towards him and his diseases is still the same. Just as the doctor had adopted a certain relation to his patient which he could not abandon, so had she formed one towards him – that he was not doing something he ought to do and was himself to blame, and that she reproached him lovingly for this – and she could not now change that attitude.

"You see he doesn't listen to me and doesn't take his medicine at the proper time. And above all he lies in a position that is no doubt bad for him – with his legs up."

She described how he made Gerasim hold his legs up.

The doctor smiled with a contemptuous affability that said: "What's to be done? These sick people do have foolish fancies of that kind, but we must forgive them."

When the examination was over the doctor looked at his watch, and then Praskovya Fedorovna announced to Ivan Ilych that it was of course as he pleased, but she had sent today for a celebrated specialist who would examine him and have a consultation with Michael Danilovich (their regular doctor).

"Please don't raise any objections. I am doing this for my own sake," she said ironically, letting it be felt that she was doing it all for his sake and only said this to leave him no right to refuse. He remained silent, knitting his brows. He felt that he was surrounded and involved in a mesh of falsity that it was hard to unravel anything.

Everything she did for him was entirely for her own sake, and she told him she was doing for herself what she actually was doing for herself, as if that was so incredible that he must understand the opposite.

At half– past eleven the celebrated specialist arrived. Again the sounding began and the significant conversations in his presence and in another room, about the kidneys and the appendix, and the questions and answers, with such an air of importance that again, instead of the real question of life and death which now alone confronted him, the question arose of the kidney and appendix which were not behaving as they ought to and would now be attached by Michael Danilovich and the specialist and forced to amend their ways.

The celebrated specialist took leave of him with a serious though not hopeless look, and in reply to the timid question Ivan Ilych, with eyes glistening with fear and hope, put to him as to whether there was a chance of recovery, said that he could not vouch for it but there was a possibility. The look of hope with which Ivan Ilych watched the doctor out was so pathetic that Praskovya Fedorovna, seeing it, even wept as she left the room to hand the doctor his fee.

The gleam of hope kindled by the doctor's encouragement did not last long. The same room, the same pictures, curtains, wall– paper, medicine bottles, were all there, and the same aching suffering body, and Ivan Ilych began to moan. They gave him a subcutaneous injection and he sank into oblivion.

It was twilight when he came to. They brought him his dinner and he swallowed some beef tea with difficulty, and then everything was the same again and night was coming on.

After dinner, at seven o'clock, Praskovya Fedorovna came into the room in evening dress, her full bosom pushed up by her corset, and with traces of powder on her face. She had reminded him in the morning that they were going to the theatre. Sarah Bernhardt was visiting the town and they had a box, which he had insisted on their taking. Now he had forgotten about it and her toilet offended him, but he concealed his vexation when he remembered that he had himself insisted on their securing a box and going because it would be an instructive and aesthetic pleasure for the children.

Praskovya Fedorovna came in, self– satisfied but yet with a rather guilty air. She sat down and asked how he was, but, as he saw, only for the sake of asking and not in order to learn about it, knowing that there was nothing to learn – and then went on to what she really wanted to say: that she would not on any account have gone but that the box had been taken and Helen and their daughter were going, as well as Petrishchev (the examining magistrate, their daughter's fiance) and that it was out of the question to let them go alone; but that she would have much preferred to sit with him for a while; and he must be sure to follow the doctor's orders while she was away.

"Oh, and Fedor Petrovich" (the fiance) "would like to come in. May he? And Lisa?"

"All right."

Their daughter came in in full evening dress, her fresh young flesh exposed (making a show of that very flesh which in his own case caused so much suffering), strong, healthy, evidently in love, and impatient with illness, suffering, and death, because they interfered with her happiness.

Fedor petrovich came in too, in evening dress, his hair curled a la Capoul , a tight stiff collar round his long sinewy neck, an enormous white shirt– front and narrow black trousers tightly stretched over his strong thighs. He had one white glove tightly drawn on, and was holding his opera hat in his hand.

Following him the schoolboy crept in unnoticed, in a new uniform, poor little fellow, and wearing gloves. Terribly dark shadows showed under his eyes, the meaning of which Ivan Ilych knew well.

His son had always seemed pathetic to him, and now it was dreadful to see the boy's frightened look of pity. It seemed to Ivan Ilych that Vasya was the only one besides Gerasim who understood and pitied him.

They all sat down and again asked how he was. A silence followed. Lisa asked her mother about the opera glasses, and there was an altercation between mother and daughter as to who had taken them and where they had been put. This occasioned some unpleasantness.

Fedor Petrovich inquired of Ivan Ilych whether he had ever seen Sarah Bernhardt. Ivan Ilych did not at first catch the question, but then replied: "No, have you seen her before?"

"Yes, in Adrienne Lecouvreur ."

Praskovya Fedorovna mentioned some roles in which Sarah Bernhardt was particularly good. Her daughter disagreed. Conversation sprang up as to the elegance and realism of her acting – the sort of conversation that is always repeated and is always the same.

In the midst of the conversation Fedor Petrovich glanced at Ivan Ilych and became silent. The others also looked at him and grew silent. Ivan Ilych was staring with glittering eyes straight before him, evidently indignant with them. This had to be rectified, but it was impossible to do so. The silence had to be broken, but for a time no one dared to break it and they all became afraid that the conventional deception would suddenly become obvious and the truth become plain to all. Lisa was the first to pluck up courage and break that silence, but by trying to hide what everybody was feeling, she betrayed it.

"Well, if we are going it's time to start," she said, looking at her watch, a present from her father, and with a faint and significant smile at Fedor Petrovich relating to something known only to them. She got up with a rustle of her dress.

They all rose, said good– night, and went away.

When they had gone it seemed to Ivan Ilych that he felt better; the falsity had gone with them. But the pain remained – that same pain and that same fear that made everything monotonously alike, nothing harder and nothing easier. Everything was worse.

Again minute followed minute and hour followed hour. Everything remained the same and there was no cessation. And the inevitable end of it all became more and more terrible.

"Yes, send Gerasim here," he replied to a question Peter asked.

CHAPTER IX

His wife returned late at night. She came in on tiptoe, but he heard her, opened his eyes, and made haste to close them again. She wished to send Gerasim away and to sit with him herself, but he opened his eyes and said: "No, go away."

"Are you in great pain?"

"Always the same."

"Take some opium."

He agreed and took some. She went away.

Till about three in the morning he was in a state of stupefied misery. It seemed to him that he and his pain were being thrust into a narrow, deep black sack, but though they were pushed further and further in they could not be pushed to the bottom. And this, terrible enough in itself, was accompanied by suffering. He was frightened yet wanted to fall through the sack, he struggled but yet co– operated. And suddenly he broke through, fell, and regained consciousness. Gerasim was sitting at the foot of the bed dozing quietly and patiently, while he himself lay with his emaciated stockinged legs resting on Gerasim's shoulders; the same shaded candle was there and the same unceasing pain.

"Go away, Gerasim," he whispered.

"It's all right, sir. I'll stay a while."

"No. Go away."

He removed his legs from Gerasim's shoulders, turned sideways onto his arm, and felt sorry for himself. He only waited till Gerasim had gone into the next room and then restrained himself no longer but wept like a child. He wept on account of his helplessness, his terrible loneliness, the cruelty of man, the cruelty of God, and the absence of God.

"Why hast Thou done all this? Why hast Thou brought me here? Why, why dost Thou torment me so terribly?"

He did not expect an answer and yet wept because there was no answer and could be none. The pain again grew more acute, but he did not stir and did not call. He said to himself: "Go on! Strike me! But what is it for? What have I done to Thee? What is it for?"

Then he grew quiet and not only ceased weeping but even held his breath and became all attention. It was as though he were listening not to an audible voice but to the voice of his soul, to the current of thoughts arising within him.

"What is it you want?" was the first clear conception capable of expression in words, that he heard.

"What do you want? What do you want?" he repeated to himself.

"What do I want? To live and not to suffer," he answered.

And again he listened with such concentrated attention that even his pain did not distract him.

"To live? How?" asked his inner voice.

"Why, to live as I used to – well and pleasantly."

"As you lived before, well and pleasantly?" the voice repeated.

And in imagination he began to recall the best moments of his pleasant life. But strange to say none of those best moments of his pleasant life now seemed at all what they had then seemed – none of them except the first recollections of childhood. There, in childhood, there had been something really pleasant with which it would be possible to live if it could return. But the child who had experienced that happiness existed no longer, it was like a reminiscence of somebody else. as soon as the period began which had produced the present Ivan Ilych, all that had then seemed joys now melted before his sight and turned into something trivial and often nasty.

And the further he departed from childhood and the nearer he came to the present the more worthless and doubtful were the joys. This began with the School of Law. A little that was really good was still found there – there was lightheartedness, friendship, and hope. But in the upper classes there had already been fewer of such good moments. Then during the first years of his official career, when he was in the service of the governor, some pleasant moments again occurred: they were the memories of love for a woman. Then all became confused and there was still less of what was good; later on again there was still less that was good, and the further he went the less there was. His marriage, a mere accident, then the disenchantment that followed it, his wife's bad breath and the sensuality and hypocrisy: then that deadly official life and those preoccupations about money, a year of it, and two, and ten, and twenty, and always the same thing. And the longer it lasted the more deadly it became. "It is as if I had been going downhill while I imagined I was going up. And that is really what it was. I was going up in public opinion, but to the same extent life was ebbing away from me. And now it is all done and there is only death.

"Then what does it mean? Why? It can't be that life is so senseless and horrible. But if it really has been so horrible and senseless, why must I die and die in agony? There is something wrong!

"Maybe I did not live as I ought to have done," it suddenly occurred to him. "But how could that be, when I did everything properly?" he replied, and immediately dismissed from his mind this, the sole solution of all the riddles of life and death, as something quite impossible.

"Then what do you want now? To live? Live how? Live as you lived in the law courts when the usher proclaimed 'The judge is coming!' The judge is coming, the judge!" he repeated to himself. "Here he is, the judge. But I am not guilty!" he exclaimed angrily. "What is it for?" And he ceased crying, but turning his face to the wall continued to ponder on the same question: Why, and for what purpose, is there all this horror? But however much he pondered he found no answer. And whenever the thought occurred to him, as it often did, that it all resulted from his not having lived as he ought to have done, he at once recalled the correctness of his whole life and dismissed so strange an idea.

Chapter X

Another fortnight passed. Ivan Ilych now no longer left his sofa. He would not lie in bed but lay on the sofa, facing the wall nearly all the time. He suffered ever the same unceasing agonies and in his loneliness pondered always on the same insoluble question: "What is this? Can it be that it is Death?" And the inner voice answered: "Yes, it is Death."

"Why these sufferings?" And the voice answered, "For no reason – they just are so." Beyond and besides this there was nothing.

From the very beginning of his illness, ever since he had first been to see the doctor, Ivan Ilych's life had been divided between two contrary and alternating moods: now it was despair and the expectation of this uncomprehended and terrible death, and now hope and an intently interested observation of the functioning of his organs. Now before his eyes there was only a kidney or an intestine that temporarily evaded its duty, and now only that incomprehensible and dreadful death from which it was impossible to escape.

These two states of mind had alternated from the very beginning of his illness, but the further it progressed the more doubtful and fantastic became the conception of the kidney, and the more real the sense of impending death.

He had but to call to mind what he had been three months before and what he was now, to call to mind with what regularity he had been going downhill, for every possibility of hope to be shattered.

Latterly during the loneliness in which he found himself as he lay facing the back of the sofa, a loneliness in the midst of a populous town and surrounded by numerous acquaintances and relations but that yet could not have been more complete anywhere – either at the bottom of the sea or under the earth – during that terrible loneliness Ivan ilych had lived only in memories of the past. Pictures of his past rose before him one after another. they always began with what was nearest in time and then went back to what was most remote – to his childhood – and rested there. If he thought of the stewed prunes that had been offered him that day, his mind went back to the raw shrivelled French plums of his childhood, their peculiar flavour and the flow of saliva when he sucked their stones, and along with the memory of that taste came a whole series of memories of those days: his nurse, his brother, and their toys. "No, I mustn't thing of that....It is too painful," Ivan Ilych said to himself, and brought himself back to the present – to the button on the back of the sofa and the creases in its morocco. "Morocco is expensive, but it does not wear well: there had been a quarrel about it. It was a different kind of quarrel and a different kind of morocco that time when we tore father's portfolio and were punished, and mamma brought us some tarts...." And again his thoughts dwelt on his childhood, and again it was painful and he tried to banish them and fix his mind on something else.

Then again together with that chain of memories another series passed through his mind – of how his illness had progressed and grown worse. There also the further back he looked the more life there had been. There had been more of what was good in life and more of life itself. The two merged together. "Just as the pain went on getting worse and worse, so my life grew worse and worse," he thought. "There is one bright spot there at the back, at the beginning of life, and afterwards all becomes blacker and blacker and proceeds more and more rapidly – in inverse ration to the square of the distance from death," thought Ivan Ilych. And the example of a stone falling downwards with increasing velocity entered his mind. Life, a series of increasing sufferings, flies further and further towards its end – the most terrible suffering. "I am flying...." He shuddered, shifted himself, and tried to resist, but was already aware that resistance was impossible, and again with eyes weary of gazing but unable to cease seeing what was before them, he stared at the back of the sofa and waited – awaiting that dreadful fall and shock and destruction.

"Resistance is impossible!" he said to himself. "If I could only understand what it is all for! But that too is impossible. An explanation would be possible if it could be said that I have not lived as I ought to. But it is impossible to say that," and he remembered all the legality, correctitude, and propriety of his life. "That at any rate can certainly not be admitted," he thought, and his lips smiled ironically as if someone could see that smile and be taken in by it. "There is no explanation! Agony, death.... What for?"

CHAPTER XI

Another two weeks went by in this way and during that fortnight an even occurred that Ivan Ilych and his wife had desired. Petrishchev formally proposed. It happened in the evening. The next day Praskovya Fedorovna came into her husband's room considering how best to inform him of it, but that very night there had been a fresh change for the worse in his condition. She found him still lying on the sofa but in a different position. He lay on his back, groaning and staring fixedly straight in front of him.

She began to remind him of his medicines, but he turned his eyes towards her with such a look that she did not finish what she was saying; so great an animosity, to her in particular, did that look express.

"For Christ's sake let me die in peace!" he said.

She would have gone away, but just then their daughter came in and went up to say good morning. He looked at her as he had done at his wife, and in reply to her inquiry about his health said dryly that he would soon free them all of himself. They were both silent and after sitting with him for a while went away.

"Is it our fault?" Lisa said to her mother. "It's as if we were to blame! I am sorry for papa, but why should we be tortured?"

The doctor came at his usual time. Ivan Ilych answered "Yes" and "No," never taking his angry eyes from him, and at last said: "You know you can do nothing for me, so leave me alone."

"We can ease your sufferings."

"You can't even do that. Let me be."

The doctor went into the drawing room and told Praskovya Fedorovna that the case was very serious and that the only resource left was opium to allay her husband's sufferings, which must be terrible.

It was true, as the doctor said, that Ivan Ilych's physical sufferings were terrible, but worse than the physical sufferings were his mental sufferings which were his chief torture.

His mental sufferings were due to the fact that that night, as he looked at Gerasim's sleepy, good– natured face with it prominent cheek– bones, the question suddenly occurred to him: "What if my whole life has been wrong?"

It occurred to him that what had appeared perfectly impossible before, namely that he had not spent his life as he should have done, might after all be true. It occurred to him that his scarcely perceptible attempts to struggle against what was considered good by the most highly placed people, those scarcely noticeable impulses which he had immediately suppressed, might have been the real thing, and all the rest false. And his professional duties and the whole arrangement of his life and of his family, and all his social and official interests, might all have been false. He tried to defend all those things to himself and suddenly felt the weakness of what he was defending. There was nothing to defend.

"But if that is so," he said to himself, "and i am leaving this life with the consciousness that I have lost all that was given me and it is impossible to rectify it – what then?"

He lay on his back and began to pass his life in review in quite a new way. In the morning when he saw first his footman, then his wife, then his daughter, and then the doctor, their every word and movement confirmed to him the awful truth that had been revealed to him during the night. In them he saw himself – all that for which he had lived – and saw clearly that it was not real at all, but a terrible and huge deception which had hidden both life and death. This consciousness intensified his physical suffering tenfold. He groaned and tossed about, and pulled at his clothing which choked and stifled him. And he hated them on that account.

He was given a large dose of opium and became unconscious, but at noon his sufferings began again. He drove everybody away and tossed from side to side.

His wife came to him and said:

"Jean, my dear, do this for me. It can't do any harm and often helps. Healthy people often do it."

He opened his eyes wide.

"What? Take communion? Why? It's unnecessary! However..."

She began to cry.

"Yes, do, my dear. I'll send for our priest. He is such a nice man."

"All right. Very well," he muttered.

When the priest came and heard his confession, Ivan Ilych was softened and seemed to feel a relief from his doubts and consequently from his sufferings, and for a moment there came a ray of hope. He again began to think of the vermiform appendix and the possibility of correcting it. He received the sacrament with tears in his eyes.

When they laid him down again afterwards he felt a moment's ease, and the hope that he might live awoke in him again. He began to think of the operation that had been suggested to him. "To live! I want to live!" he said to himself.

His wife came in to congratulate him after his communion, and when uttering the usual conventional words she added:

"You feel better, don't you?"

Without looking at her he said "Yes."

Her dress, her figure, the expression of her face, the tone of her voice, all revealed the same thing. "This is wrong, it is not as it should be. All you have lived for and still live for is falsehood and deception, hiding life and death from you." And as soon as he admitted that thought, his hatred and his agonizing physical suffering again sprang up, and with that suffering a consciousness of the unavoidable, approaching end. And to this was added a new sensation of grinding shooting pain and a feeling of suffocation.

The expression of his face when he uttered that "Yes" was dreadful. Having uttered it, he looked her straight in the eyes, turned on his face with a rapidity extraordinary in his weak state and shouted:

"Go away! Go away and leave me alone!"

Chapter XII

From that moment the screaming began that continued for three days, and was so terrible that one could not hear it through two closed doors without horror. At the moment he answered his wife realized that he was lost, that there was no return, that the end had come, the very end, and his doubts were still unsolved and remained doubts.

"Oh! Oh! Oh!" he cried in various intonations. He had begun by screaming "I won't!" and continued screaming on the letter "O".

For three whole days, during which time did not exist for him, he struggled in that black sack into which he was being thrust by an invisible, resistless force. He struggled as a man condemned to death struggles in the hands of the executioner, knowing that he cannot save himself. And every moment he felt that despite all his efforts he was drawing nearer and nearer to what terrified him. he felt that his agony was due to his being thrust into that black hole and still more to his not being able to get right into it. He was hindered from getting into it by his conviction that his life had been a good one. That very justification of his life held him fast and prevented his moving forward, and it caused him most torment of all.

Suddenly some force struck him in the chest and side, making it still harder to breathe, and he fell through the hole and there at the bottom was a light. What had happened to him was like the sensation one sometimes experiences in a railway carriage when one thinks one is going backwards while one is really going forwards and suddenly becomes aware of the real direction.

"Yes, it was not the right thing," he said to himself, "but that's no matter. It can be done. But what is the right thing? he asked himself, and suddenly grew quiet.

This occurred at the end of the third day, two hours before his death. Just then his schoolboy son had crept softly in and gone up to the bedside. The dying man was still screaming desperately and waving his arms. His hand fell on the boy's head, and the boy caught it, pressed it to his lips, and began to cry.

At that very moment Ivan Ilych fell through and caught sight of the light, and it was revealed to him that though his life had not been what it should have been, this could still be rectified. He asked himself, "What is the right thing?" and grew still, listening. Then he felt that someone was kissing his hand. He opened his eyes, looked at his son, and felt sorry for him. His wife camp up to him and he glanced at her. She was gazing at him open– mouthed, with undried tears on her nose and cheek and a despairing look on her face. He felt sorry for her too.

"Yes, I am making them wretched," he thought. "They are sorry, but it will be better for them when I die." He wished to say this but had not the strength to utter it. "Besides, why speak? I must act," he thought. with a look at his wife he indicated his son and said: "Take him away...sorry for him...sorry for you too...." He tried to add, "Forgive me," but said "Forego" and waved his hand, knowing that He whose understanding mattered would understand.

And suddenly it grew clear to him that what had been oppressing him and would not leave his was all dropping away at once from two sides, from ten sides, and from all sides. He was sorry for them, he must act so as not to hurt them: release them and free himself from these sufferings. "How good and how simple!" he thought. "And the pain?" he asked himself. "What has become of it? Where are you, pain?"

He turned his attention to it.

"Yes, here it is. Well, what of it? Let the pain be."

"And death...where is it?"

He sought his former accustomed fear of death and did not find it. "Where is it? What death?" There was no fear because there was no death.

In place of death there was light.

"So that's what it is!" he suddenly exclaimed aloud. "What joy!"

To him all this happened in a single instant, and the meaning of that instant did not change. For those present his agony continued for another two hours. Something rattled in his throat, his emaciated body twitched, then the gasping and rattle became less and less frequent.

"It is finished!" said someone near him.

He heard these words and repeated them in his soul.

"Death is finished," he said to himself. "It is no more!"

He drew in a breath, stopped in the midst of a sigh, stretched out, and died.

Alyosha the Pot

Alyosha was the younger brother. He was called the Pot, because his mother had once sent him with a pot of milk to the deacon's wife, and he had stumbled against something and broken it. His mother had beaten him, and the children had teased him. Since then he was nicknamed the Pot. Alyosha was a tiny, thin little fellow, with ears like wings, and a huge nose. "Alyosha has a nose that looks like a dog on a hill!" the children used to call after him. Alyosha went to the village school, but was not good at lessons; besides, there was so little time to learn. His elder brother was in town, working for a merchant, so Alyosha had to help his father from a very early age. When he was no more than six he used to go out with the girls to watch the cows and sheep in the pasture, and a little later he looked after the horses by day and by night. And at twelve years of age he had already begun to plough and to drive the cart. The skill was there though the strength was not. He was always cheerful. Whenever the children made fun of him, he would either laugh or be silent. When his father scolded him he would stand mute and listen attentively, and as soon as the scolding was over would smile and go on with his work. Alyosha was nineteen when his brother was taken as a soldier. So his father placed him with the merchant as a yard– porter. He was given his brother's old boots, his father's old coat and cap, and was taken to town. Alyosha was delighted with his clothes, but the merchant was not impressed by his appearance.

"I thought you would bring me a man in Simeon's place," he said, scanning Alyosha; "and you've brought me THIS! What's the good of him?"

"He can do everything; look after horses and drive. He's a good one to work. He looks rather thin, but he's tough enough. And he's very willing."

"He looks it. All right; we'll see what we can do with him."

So Alyosha remained at the merchant's.

The family was not a large one. It consisted of the merchant's wife: her old mother: a married son poorly educated who was in his father's business: another son, a learned one who had finished school and entered the University, but having been expelled, was living at home: and a daughter who still went to school.

They did not take to Alyosha at first. He was uncouth, badly dressed, and had no manner, but they soon got used to him. Alyosha worked even better than his brother had done; he was really very willing. They sent him on all sorts of errands, but he did everything quickly and readily, going from one task to another without stopping. And so here, just as at home, all the work was put upon his shoulders. The more he did, the more he was given to do. His mistress, her old mother, the son, the daughter, the clerk, and the cook– all ordered him about, and sent him from one place to another.

"Alyosha, do this! Alyosha, do that! What! have you forgotten, Alyosha? Mind you don't forget, Alyosha!" was heard from morning till night. And Alyosha ran here, looked after this and that, forgot nothing, found time for everything, and was always cheerful.

His brother's old boots were soon worn out, and his master scolded him for going about in tatters with his toes sticking out. He ordered another pair to be bought for him in the market. Alyosha was delighted with his new boots, but was angry with his feet when they ached at the end of the day after so much running about. And then he was afraid that his father would be annoyed when he came to town for his wages, to find that his master had deducted the cost of the boots.

In the winter Alyosha used to get up before daybreak. He would chop the wood, sweep the yard, feed the cows and horses, light the stoves, clean the boots, prepare the samovars and polish them afterwards; or the clerk would get him to bring up the goods; or the cook would set him to knead the bread and clean the saucepans. Then he was sent to town on various errands, to bring the daughter home from school, or to get some olive oil for the old mother. "Why the devil have you been so long?" first one, then another, would say to him. Why should they go? Alyosha can go. "Alyosha! Alyosha!" And Alyosha ran here and there. He breakfasted in snatches while he was working, and rarely managed to get his dinner at the proper hour. The cook used to scold him for being late, but she was sorry for him all the same, and would keep something hot for his dinner and supper.

At holiday times there was more work than ever, but Alyosha liked holidays because everybody gave him a tip. Not much certainly, but it would amount up to about sixty kopeks [1s 2d]– his very own money. For Alyosha never set eyes on his wages. His father used to come and take them from the merchant, and only scold Alyosha for wearing out his boots.

When he had saved up two roubles [4s], by the advice of the cook he bought himself a red knitted jacket, and was so happy when he put it on, that he couldn't close his mouth for joy. Alyosha was not talkative; when he spoke at all, he spoke abruptly, with his head turned away. When told to do anything, or asked if he could do it, he would say yes without the smallest hesitation, and set to work at once.

Alyosha did not know any prayer; and had forgotten what his mother had taught him. But he prayed just the same, every morning and every evening, prayed with his hands, crossing himself.

He lived like this for about a year and a half, and towards the end of the second year a most startling thing happened to him. He discovered one day, to his great surprise, that, in addition to the relation of usefulness existing between people, there was also another, a peculiar relation of quite a different character. Instead of a man being wanted to clean boots, and go on errands and harness horses, he is not wanted to be of any service at all, but another human being wants to serve him and pet him. Suddenly Alyosha felt he was such a man.

He made this discovery through the cook Ustinia. She was young, had no parents, and worked as hard as Alyosha. He felt for the first time in his life that he– not his services, but he himself– was necessary to another human being. When his mother used to be sorry for him, he had taken no notice of her. It had seemed to him quite natural, as though he were feeling sorry for himself. But here was Ustinia, a perfect stranger, and sorry for him. She would save him some hot porridge, and sit watching him, her chin propped on her bare arm, with the sleeve rolled up, while he was eating it. When he looked at her she would begin to laugh, and he would laugh too.

This was such a new, strange thing to him that it frightened Alyosha. He feared that it might interfere with his work. But he was pleased, nevertheless, and when he glanced at the trousers that Ustinia had mended for him, he would shake his head and smile. He would often think of her while at work, or when running on errands. "A fine girl, Ustinia!" he sometimes exclaimed.

Ustinia used to help him whenever she could, and he helped her. She told him all about her life; how she had lost her parents; how her aunt had taken her in and found a place for her in the town; how the merchant's son had tried to take liberties with her, and how she had rebuffed him. She liked to talk, and Alyosha liked to listen to her. He had heard that peasants who came up to work in the towns frequently got married to servant girls. On one occasion she asked him if his parents intended marrying him soon. He said that he did not know; that he did not want to marry any of the village girls.

"Have you taken a fancy to some one, then?"

"I would marry you, if you'd be willing."

"Get along with you, Alyosha the Pot; but you've found your tongue, haven't you?" she exclaimed, slapping him on the back with a towel she held in her hand. "Why shouldn't I?"

At Shrovetide Alyosha's father came to town for his wages. It had come to the ears of the merchant's wife that Alyosha wanted to marry Ustinia, and she disapproved of it. "What will be the use of her with a baby?" she thought, and informed her husband.

The merchant gave the old man Alyosha's wages.

"How is my lad getting on?" he asked. "I told you he was willing."

"That's all right, as far as it goes, but he's taken some sort of nonsense into his head. He wants to marry our cook. Now I don't approve of married servants. We won't have them in the house."

"Well, now, who would have thought the fool would think of such a thing?" the old man exclaimed. "But don't you worry. I'll soon settle that."

He went into the kitchen, and sat down at the table waiting for his son. Alyosha was out on an errand, and came back breathless.

"I thought you had some sense in you; but what's this you've taken into your head?" his father began.

"I? Nothing."

"How, nothing? They tell me you want to get married. You shall get married when the time comes. I'll find you a decent wife, not some town hussy."

His father talked and talked, while Alyosha stood still and sighed. When his father had quite finished, Alyosha smiled.

"All right. I'll drop it."

"Now that's what I call sense."

When he was left alone with Ustinia he told her what his father had said. (She had listened at the door.)

"It's no good; it can't come off. Did you hear? He was angry— won't have it at any price."

Ustinia cried into her apron.

Alyosha shook his head.

"What's to be done? We must do as we're told."

"Well, are you going to give up that nonsense, as your father told you?" his mistress asked, as he was putting up the shutters in the evening.

"To be sure we are," Alyosha replied with a smile, and then burst into tears.

From that day Alyosha went about his work as usual, and no longer talked to Ustinia about their getting married. One day in Lent the clerk told him to clear the snow from the roof. Alyosha climbed on to the roof and swept away all the snow; and, while he was still raking out some frozen lumps from the gutter, his foot slipped and he fell over. Unfortunately he did not fall on the snow, but on a piece of iron over the door. Ustinia came running up, together with the merchant's daughter.

"Have you hurt yourself, Alyosha?"

"Ah! no, it's nothing."

But he could not raise himself when he tried to, and began to smile.

He was taken into the lodge. The doctor arrived, examined him, and asked where he felt the pain.

"I feel it all over," he said. "But it doesn't matter. I'm only afraid master will be annoyed. Father ought to be told."

Alyosha lay in bed for two days, and on the third day they sent for the priest.

"Are you really going to die?" Ustinia asked.

"Of course I am. You can't go on living for ever. You must go when the time comes." Alyosha spoke rapidly as usual. "Thank you, Ustinia. You've been very good to me. What a lucky thing they didn't let us marry! Where should we have been now? It's much better as it is."

When the priest came, he prayed with his bands and with his heart. "As it is good here when you obey and do no harm to others, so it will be there," was the thought within it.

He spoke very little; he only said he was thirsty, and he seemed full of wonder at something.

He lay in wonderment, then stretched himself, and died.

9 786599 154997

Printed at Repro India Ltd.